ONLY THE BROKEN REMAIN

DAN COXON

Only the
Broken
Remain

by

Dan Coxon

BLACK
SHUCK
BOOKS

Black Shuck Books

www.blackshuckbooks.co.uk

First published in Great Britain in 2020 by

Black Shuck Books

Kent, UK

Versions of the following stories have previously appeared in print:

'Stanislav in Foxtown' in *Black Static, #56* (2017, as Ian Steadman)

'Only the Broken Remain' in *The British Fantasy Society Bulletin* (2017, as Ian Steadman)

'Feather and Twine' in *Night Light* (Midnight Street Press, 2018, as Ian Steadman)

'Baddavine' in *Nightscript, Vol VI* (2020)

'Far From Home' in *Nox Pareidolia* (Nightscape Press, 2019)

'Foreign Land' in *The Lonely Crowd, Issue 5* (2016, as Ian Steadman)

'Ones and Zeros' in *The Ghastling, Issue 10* (2019)

'No One's Child' in *Not One Of Us, #63* (2020)

'Rut' in *Humanagerie* (Eibonvale Press, 2018)

'After the Reservoir' in *BFS Horizons, #9* (2019)

'All the Letters in His Van' on *unsungstories.co.uk* (2017, as Ian Steadman)

Cover and interior design © WHITEspace, 2020

www.white-space.uk

978-1-913038-59-5

STANISLAV IN FOXTOWN

At night, lying in my bed, I sometimes fantasise about murdering Mr Sharples. If he were less imposing I might strike out, solving with violence what I can't verbalise in my clumsy English. But Mr Sharples isn't the kind of man you start a fight with. His hair is cut close to his head, his nose swerves left towards a stubbled cheek. His polo shirt stretches tight over his chest, the stitched puma leaping across his pectoral muscle as if it's scaling a mountain. Next to him, I look as if I am built of chicken bones. My arms are thin like twigs, my ribs visible like a brittle hand stretched across my chest. Loose flaps of skin hang under my arms.

This life is not what I hoped for. My house – yes, I have a house – clings to the better end of the Marsh Estate. It has glass in three of its five windows. The other two are taped up with plastic sheeting that cracks and billows like sails in the wind. The living room is comfortable as long as you ignore the black bloom of mould across one corner of the ceiling. The shower squeezes out little more than a miserable trickle, but the bath is wide and deep. It is in this bath that I soak for an hour each night, topping up the hot water when it grows too cold, eyes half-closed against the cobwebs and the cracks. It is the only way to get rid of the stink of the chicken fat, and even then it sometimes lingers. My red-brown hair has become so lank that it looks almost black. When I step out of the water I see iridescent ripples on the surface.

'Stan, no slacking today,' Mr Sharples says every morning, as he wipes a steel brush around the edges of the fryer. 'I don't pay you to stand around gawping. No one in this country ever made it by staring into space, you hear me? We like to work you here. If you want a roof over your head, you have to earn it.'

I want to say that my roof is missing more tiles than I can count, that the morning after a storm I find new puddles of damp on the bedroom ceiling, terracotta shards spiking my front yard – but the words never come. On the hairy middle finger of his right hand, Mr Sharples wears a silver signet ring in the shape of a British Bulldog. I once saw what looked like dried blood in the cracks of its mouth and its eyes. I think of it splitting the skin of my cheek, leaving its animal imprint on my flesh. It is enough to make me swallow my discontent. I nod, bending my back into the work. My hands are covered with small wounds from the oil splatter, the worst of them a festering sore the size of a one-pound coin. When I look at them, it is easy to imagine that I might have some terrible disease, a resurgent medieval plague. Perhaps this is how chickenpox earned its name.

I've lost track of how long I have worked at The Fried Chicken Coop. I send money back every week, to my family in the old country. My life has degenerated into a seven-day cycle, repeating on an endless loop. Months, years, have lost their meaning. All that marks the turning of another week is my Monday night off work, the only time I have to try and build myself a life in this strange land. I use it to sleep, mostly. Sometimes I remember to eat.

On the days that I work, my meals are supplied for me. Mr Sharples calls it a 'perk'. After the last customer has ordered their greasy tub of chicken pieces, after the last table has been cleared, I fry us each a bucket to take home. Then Mr Sharples has me carry the bags of trash outside while he counts the takings. 'Drop them in the bins, not on the side,' he shouts every night, 'and make sure the lid is back on after. There's vermin round here like you wouldn't believe. Or I dunno, maybe you would.' I always do as I'm told, but still the man makes a point of saying it every night, as if I am an idiot. It makes my teeth clench, trying to keep the anger in. I walk home stinking of chicken fat, clutching my box of greasy meat, thumping my feet into the broken pavements. My fingers worry the blisters on my hands until they bleed.

It is on one of these late-night walks that I first see the animal. It slinks from behind a wall on Beech Crescent, its head down to the ground, its tail tucked low. Something makes it notice me and it stops. Maybe it is the smell. It raises its sharp, wedge-shaped muzzle and stares, trying to work out what this man who stinks of chicken is doing on its estate. It looks more confused than scared. It's the size of a medium dog, I think, but it seems smarter. And bold. Its fur is almost brown but with a hint of copper, as if there is a fire burning somewhere deep within it. The flash of white on its muzzle makes it look as if it's been stealing cream. When I move forward it holds its ground. It is only when I get within five or six feet – close enough to see the dark intelligence behind its glassy eyes – that it finally turns and darts behind the wall.

As I unlock my front door I look back at the street and there it is again, standing in the middle of the road, watching. Once I am inside I peer through the window. I try to take a photo on my phone, to send home to my family, but the exposure is so bad that all it captures is darkness. I get no signal here anyway. I have tried and tried, holding the phone out of windows, walking the streets with my eyes on the bars. Sometimes there will be a glimmer of life, but as soon as it starts to connect it vanishes again, the signal nothing more than a ghost among the estate's abandoned houses.

The animal watches my home for a couple of minutes, then it seems to be satisfied with something. It turns and strolls in the direction of the common.

The next day I ask Mr Sharples about the animal. My words aren't yet good enough to describe it, so I draw a picture in biro on the back of a napkin. That arrow-shaped head, the barely-tamed brush of a tail.

'That's a fox,' Mr Sharples tells me, his back turned as he unloads a new bag of chicken pieces from the freezer. 'You don't have those back in wherever? It's all we bloody have around here. They're taking over the estate, now that most of it's emptying out. They root through the bins.'

I remember foxes from home, but they were not like this creature. What I remember of them was scrawnier, wilder. They were animals of the woods, the heath; not the city. This seems something new. Something bolder.

Mr Sharples gives stricter instructions than usual when I put out the trash bags tonight, telling me to weight the bin lids down with bricks. I find some in a pile where the tarmac turns to dirt, the ruins of a building project that never happened. They feel dry and old in my well-greased palms. Before putting them in place I rest them against the side of the bin, and with shaking hands I untie one of the black sacks. Inside is a nest of cardboard and bones, the occasional slippery scrap of skin. Without really knowing why, I begin to fill my pockets, picking over the remains for the bones, the half-eaten corpses of wings and thighs. My jacket bulges with finger-sized bones, clusters of gristle and skin, monuments to the devoured dead. I wipe my hands on a used napkin then close the bag up again, thudding the bricks onto the bin lid.

I am disappointed not to see the animal – the fox – on my way home. I feel sure it must be out there in the darkness somewhere, beyond the pale circles of fluorescent light, sniffing at the scent of bone and meat that leaks from my coat. If it is there, it doesn't show itself. I don't know what to do with the scraps once I reach my door, so I pile them in the middle of the cement yard, a tiny cairn of dead parts. From a crack in the concrete I pick a young dandelion, chewing one of the leaves as I walk inside. It feels bold to be eating something green again, something other than oily white flesh. It tastes bitter and metallic, like old blood. As I gnaw on my lukewarm chicken dinner, as I prepare for bed, as I brush my teeth, I glance out from time to time, but the pile is always still there. After my bath I give it one final check, then I turn in for the night.

In the morning, the bones are gone.

I prowl around the yard before heading to work, finding the fine needle of a wing bone next to the fence, a knuckle of cartilage that may have been part of a thigh. The rest has disappeared. In one corner, the furthest from the house, I find a dark pile of fresh scat. There's a musky smell too, more than just the earthy stink of animal shit. I haven't owned a pet since I was a child, and something deep within me glows at the idea of nurturing this creature.

At the end of the night I fill my bucket with wings, cramming fifteen into the tub. The boniest part of the chicken. I fill my pockets again, taking a fistful of napkins out with the waste so I might wrap the bones and skin in them before hiding them in my jacket. There are already grease spots showing on the lining. One of them has leached through to the outside, a dark, oily stain that looks wet to the touch. If Mr Sharples notices it as I walk out the door, he doesn't say. Maybe he thinks I am resorting to eating the garbage.

The fox doesn't make an appearance on the walk home, but I pile the scraps in the yard anyway. I eat my wings kneeling backwards on the sofa, watching through the window. When I am done the bucket is still half full. I take it outside and add the bones, the claw-like wing tips, to the pile. Then I retreat indoors.

It comes at a few minutes past midnight, pointing its wedge-shaped muzzle around the fence. I can see it sniffing the air, then it pads across the uneven cement, its feet lifting with the precision of a dressage horse. For some reason the movement makes me think that it is a she, and I feel the urge to name her. I call her Tabitha. She sniffs the pile of bones, and for a moment I think she is going to turn around and leave. Then she lifts her head and looks at the window. I hold my breath. Her eyes stay fixed on the house as she circles, slowly, putting the pile between herself and the man behind the glass. Only then, when she is able to see the food and the human at the same time, does she start to eat.

I am almost nodding asleep when the second fox arrives. This one is bigger – a male, I guess – and its fur looks matted and ruffled in places, as if it has been wrestling something large out in the darkness. One of its ears is partly missing, ending in a jagged tear that looks like it's been bitten. Tabitha glances up then steps back from the pile. There is a hierarchy to be obeyed. Torn-ear walks forward as if she isn't there and places his paw on the bones, bending his head to the food. When she steps back to join him he looks up briefly, a scrap of skin visible in his open jaw. Then he returns to his meal. I have the feeling that I am still being watched, by both foxes now. My tiredness is becoming insistent, and as I write a text that I cannot send to my family I feel my eyelids dropping. Before they finish eating I take myself up to bed.

When I wake in the morning I realise that I didn't bathe last night, and the sheets are now scented with the greasy stink of chicken. I can taste it as my head lies on the pillow, feel it slipping through the grain of my skin. I take a towel from the laundry basket and rub it, dry, across my body, hoping to wipe the oil from me, but it makes no difference. Even my armpits smell of chicken.

The front yard is empty again, last night's meal cleared away with mechanical efficiency. I consider cleaning up the two fresh piles of scat under the window, but in the end I can't be bothered. The estate is falling into ruin. This waste ground is as much theirs as it is mine, and it occurs to me that they might claim a deeper, more ancient ownership of it than man ever could. Let them shit where they like.

Mr Sharples is in a more combative mood than usual, as if he can smell the unwashed neglect on my skin. He shouts at me when I drop a thigh on the tiled floor, then sweeps it into the fryer when the customer isn't looking. After, he tells me that the wastage will come out of my wages. *What wastage?* I want to ask. *You have still cooked it, so where is the waste?* But I stay silent, my head bent over the oil. A reduced wage is still a wage. Besides, I need the money to send back home. And my new friends need the bones.

It's as I clear the empty buckets and greasy napkins from the tables that Mr Sharples calls me over to the fryer. Bundling what I have into one of the trash sacks, I go to stand beside him. He is staring into the bubbling fat. Every few seconds a speck of something dark tumbles to the surface before disappearing again into the depths.

'You see that?' I can hear the anger in his voice. 'Down there, in the bottom. You see it? You know what that is? I'll tell you what it is. It's a wing, that's what it is. You've lost a wing down there, so that's coming out of your wages too. I've told you before, we can't afford to waste the chicken. And now we'll have to dig it out. Or rather, you will. Use the net. And if I see it again, you're paying double.'

I can't see what he is talking about, but I fetch the net anyway, dredging it through the oil until I feel something stick. Lifting it out of the fat a stray trickle slips down the handle, scalding my fingers. I almost drop it back into the vat, but I hold on. My fingers are already showing violent red welts – in the morning there will be blisters. Tipping out the net, a charred lump tumbles onto the counter. It may once have been a wing, I suppose. Wrapping it in a fistful of napkins I throw it into the waste bin.

Taking out the trash is harder tonight, the burns on my hands throbbing and raw. Lifting the bags draws tears from my eyes. It is as I lift a brick to rest it on top of the bin that I see the fox on the edge of the light, its fur like rust in the darkness. Peering closer I see there are two: Tabitha and Torn-ear. They stand patiently, watching me, their stillness born of generations of waiting. I place the brick back on the ground and walk inside.

Back home, I sit at the window again and count down the hours. They appear a little before one, arrowing confidently through the darkness, aiming for my front yard. I'm not sure whether they will have eaten already, but I have built the pile of bones and skin anyway. I know what it is like to go hungry. Torn-ear comes first, swaggering through the night like the veteran he is. He does not look but I know he senses me, I can feel his alertness reaching out, mapping his territory. Once he has started, Tabitha joins him. She is hungrier tonight, and after a while he steps back, allowing her the larger share. She is barely halfway through the pile when there's a movement on the fringes and a third fox appears – slim, younger, sleeker – then a fourth, then a fifth. The newcomers look up at my window but they do not hesitate. They already know that I don't pose a threat.

I count eleven foxes during the course of the night, some drifting away then coming back, others remaining in the yard until the tiredness gets too much for me. I don't know how long they stay. I think I hear yelping in my dreams, like feral babies stalking the derelict wasteland. I stink in my greasy sheets again the next morning. When I check the yard, all sign of them is gone.

I almost don't notice it when I open the front door. My mind is still slow and half-dreaming. At first I think it is a small rock. I go to kick it away. Then something looks familiar and I bend down. It's the nugget of chicken wing that Mr Sharples had me fish out of the fryer, the cause of the itching, burning welts on my hands. I try to think back to the night before. When nothing makes sense I pick it up and place it in my coat pocket.

On the walk to work I almost expect to see the foxes again, skulking behind gates, peering around cracked walls. If they are there, they hide better than I am able to see.

'I told you what would happen if you didn't do it right, now see what it's like?' Mr Sharples is already boiling over this morning, shouting as soon as I arrive. 'If you want a job done properly, and all that... But I trusted you Stan, and you've fucking let me down. You can clean up the mess out there, and I'm not paying you for it either. The clock starts when you get back inside, not a minute before. How hard can it be to do a simple job?'

The bins at the back of the restaurant are open, the bags ripped open and their contents scattered across the tarmac. Tattered pennants of ketchup-stained napkins fly from gnawed bones. One of the cardboard buckets has been chewed up and spat out again. I know it was the foxes. I understand the offering at my door now. There has been an alliance made between us, a contract signed in grease and sweat. It takes me almost an hour to pick up the remains of their feast, scooping their litter into new black sacks before heaving them into the bins. Somewhere, somehow, I am certain they are watching me.

Mr Sharples screams at me for most of the day, his spit flying in my face as he scolds me for not wiping the tables thoroughly, for dropping a stripped thigh bone into the oil. I'm too tired to care. I watch the bone spinning in the lake of fat, fireworks fizzing off its ends. I'm not sure whether I'm awake or dreaming.

When the time comes to take out the trash I don't bother with the bricks at all. As a test, I pull yesterday's burnt chicken wing from my pocket and place it on top of the pile, then I look for something else to leave. Something that will seal our pact. In the end I take off my shoes and peel off my socks, balling them together and leaving them next to the wing. An offering of sorts. My shoes feel cold as I slip them back on but I find that I'm smiling as I walk inside. There is no chicken in my bucket tonight, only scraps. My heels feel raw against the leather of my shoes. As I walk home along Beech Crescent, turning left onto Ashgrove, past the abandoned tenements, I drop pieces at intervals – a half-chewed wing, a knuckle of gristle, a rubbery flap of skin. I make a path leading to my front door, a trail of greasy breadcrumbs. Let them come. Let them all come.

I don't have long to wait. I was right. They have been watching. As soon as I'm inside they start to appear, one or two at a time, drawn to the bone pile like a bonfire in the darkness. Some circle it, waiting for their turn. Others don't hesitate to take what is owed to them. Torn-ear is among the first. He looks at the window where I sit as he snarls his mouth around a half-eaten thigh. I swear he nods.

I still have no signal on my phone, but I think I must record the moment somehow. There's a magic I must harness. I can't count how many foxes there are now, their ranks spilling out into the blackness. I lose count at twenty-eight. There must be at least twice that. Maybe a hundred or more. Maybe they never end. I try recording a video through the window but all I see is my own reflection, scrawny, slope-shouldered, eyes sunken and dark. I'm loath to step outside, but something leads me to the front door. I swing it open as quietly as I can.

The foxes do not run. They see me, but they do not care. They know that I pose no threat to them. I hold up my phone and press the red button, shooting a video that the world will never get to see. As I film them, three shapes push forward from the masses. I recognise Torn-ear. The other two are new to me: even older than him, their muzzles tattered and wild, their bodies lean but heavy with muscle. It's cold outside and their breath mists about them. There's an animal musk that I hadn't noticed at first, awakening ancestral memories of hollowed-out caves, nights spent shivering in the glow from a fire. As the estate crumbles around us I can't help wondering whether I'm being allowed a glimpse into the future.

One of the foxes pads forward, something in its mouth. It bends and drops the object between us, then backs up to join the others. It's the burnt chicken wing again, the offering I'd left in the bin. It looks softer now, worn away by claws and teeth as it passes back and forth between us, a primitive form of currency. A token to seal the pact.

I see now that the other two hold objects in their mouths too. Torn-ear is next, stalking towards me with a cat-like swagger, dropping my balled-up socks near my feet. He has been gentle with them. The only sign of their journey is a darkened crescent of saliva, the imprint of his teeth. I wonder if I should pick them up, if these offerings are mine to take.

Then the third steps forward. He's the biggest of the three, his fur thick and knotted in places. There are two bald patches across his back, what I imagine must be old scars. He holds my gaze as he treads slowly across the yard and I notice that his eyes are deep black, reflecting nothing back at me, sucking the world in and giving nothing in return. There's a deadness that scares me. When he opens his mouth something drops to the concrete with a dull thump, but it's only when he turns that the spell is broken and I can finally look down. At first, I'm not sure what I'm seeing. It doesn't make sense: a giant, crippled spider at my feet. Where might they have found a spider that large? It looks alien, out of place in this country of tamed animals. I imagine it crawling over a desert rock.

Then I see that the legs are not legs at all, but fingers. Thick, hairy fingers. And on the middle finger sits a signet ring in the shape of a British Bulldog, snarling at the world.

The foxes stand and watch me as I retreat inside, their numbers stretching back into the night. I stumble over the step, almost fall backwards into the hallway. An outstretched arm braces against the wall. My hand is trembling, and as I close the door I imagine them watching it, licking their lips. When I realise that I'm still clutching my phone I stop recording, delete the file. Without looking through the glass I draw the thin curtains across my windows. Run myself a bath. Then I start, with shaking hands, to wash the stink of chicken from my skin.

The next morning it takes all my resolve to leave the house. In my mind they are still waiting out there for me, the path a river of russet fur. I remember the old one, the leader, the way his eyes reflected back nothing but the night. The memory sets my hands trembling again. Without warning I recall their musk, almost gagging as it hits me. To make it as far as putting the key in the lock I have to tell myself that it was nothing but a fantasy, a trick of the light. A dream within a dream.

When I finally open the door, the yard is bare. There are no foxes. Not one. Not even a pile of scat or a dropped chicken bone to mark their passage. The socks have gone too, and the chicken wing. And, yes, the hand. In part I am relieved, but I know that what I saw was real, that I didn't imagine it. It makes me wonder what it means, this withdrawal of gifts. It makes me wonder what it all means.

I keep my eyes on the pavement as I walk to work, not daring to look around at the estate. I watch the cracks between the stones, the green tendrils of weeds pushing through from beneath. The empty houses outnumber the occupied ones now, and most of them are derelict, crumbling back to the dirt. There are plenty of places for an animal to hide. They could be watching me and I would never know. Maybe they have been watching me for a long time. I only stop once, at the corner of Ashgrove. There, on the path in front of me, sits a small dark pile of scat. It has been left in the middle of the pavement, like a warning, a beacon. They have been here. As I hurry on I know that I am not alone, that there is more than one pair of eyes watching me.

The door to The Fried Chicken Coop is unlocked. I let myself in. Peering through the window, I see no movement outside. I call for Mr Sharples. When I hear no reply, I look behind the counter. I don't know what I expect. Signs of a struggle, perhaps. A trail of blood. His dismembered corpse. But there is nothing to find, nothing to suggest anything out of the ordinary. Just empty tiles, a stack of boxes. I call again, then I walk to the back door and push it open. The bin lids are open but otherwise everything is in its place. No litter on the floor. No bones.

Standing on my toes I look inside the bins. The burnt wing and my socks are still gone. That is something, I guess. From this angle there looks to be a slight track across the concrete too, a trail in the dust, as if something heavy has been dragged away into the vacant waste ground behind us. I retreat inside and lock the door behind me.

With nothing better to do, I turn the fryers on and wait for them to heat up. It's almost noon and there will be mouths wanting feeding. I start to put on my usual apron, but then I realise that Mr Sharples is no longer here to impose this servitude on me. In the back room I find one of his polo shirts, brown, the leaping puma stitched in white on to the chest. It's far too big for me but I pull it on anyway, tucking fistfuls of it into my jeans. It hangs from my shoulders, the sleeves falling all the way down to my elbows. I know I must look ridiculous but I keep it on.

As the clock turns to noon I switch on the Open sign. While I wait for the first customer of the day I rip a piece of card from the side of one of the frozen chicken thigh boxes. I can't find any scissors, so I score it with a knife and tear it into something close to a neat rectangle. With a thick black marker I write a sign: *Help Wanted. Junior Fryer Needed to Start Immediately, Apply Within.* I stick it to the window with Blu-Tack.

Somewhere near the end of the street I think I see a flash of fur, a barely-visible streak of red. By the time my brain registers it, whatever it was has already vanished into the depths of the estate. I return to the fryers and start to cook.

ROLL UP, ROLL UP

Robbie didn't run away to join the circus. The circus came to him.

The local paper carried the ad one Saturday, beneath a notice for the Rotary lawn bowls tournament. *Looking for excitement?* it read. *Willing to learn? Circus de Sergei is looking to recruit new blood. Open interviews this Thursday, please call to book your slot.* There followed a number, and despite the fact that it seemed to have too many digits, when Robbie phoned it there was a recorded message and he left his name and contact details and then hung up.

He missed their call when it came, but they left a voicemail. The man's voice had a slight accent – Eastern Europe somewhere, perhaps, with just a hint of a nasal Aussie whine. Someone who had travelled the world, certainly. Someone who was *foreign*, but only in the most general sense. His voice was so deep that it made the tiny speaker in Robbie's phone buzz as he held it to his ear, and for a second he wondered if a bee had flown into his ear canal.

'I am returning your call regarding our advertisement,' the man said, slowly and deliberately. 'We would like to speak with you in person regarding your new position.' Robbie's heart skipped a beat, so that he almost missed the address. He was still writing it on the back of his hand when the voice wrapped up the message with, 'Please bring an old T-shirt and your most comfortable pair of shoes. We look forward to you joining us.'

Robbie replayed the message a couple of times. Admittedly, the man's intonation was odd, and he may not have been a native English speaker – but still, he couldn't shake the impression that this wasn't an interview but a settling-in of sorts, an *inauguration*. There had been no mention of pay, and that odd closing comment suggested that manual work might be involved, the kind that would mean getting his hands dirty. But that didn't bother him. It was employment, and it was a circus.

*

By the time Thursday morning came around, he was a wreck. Fortunately, he remembered the instructions as he stepped out of his flat, and he scurried back inside for his tie-dyed T-shirt (a well-intentioned but wildly inappropriate gift from his mum) and his fake Nikes.

The address he'd written down turned out to be on a wide but weed-infested access alley around the back of TK-Maxx, and he checked his hand again as he stood in front of the door. It had once been yellow, but now it was stained a disconcerting yellow-black, like it was made of mould or some kind of fungus. The surface was weathered and flakes of paint were peeling off, although it appeared to be exactly the same colour underneath. Robbie was reminded of a rotting tree.

When he lifted his hand and rapped on it with his knuckles the sound was hollow.

At first there was no sign of life, and he almost lost his bottle and sprinted back to the street corner. If he strained his hearing he thought he could just make out footsteps, though, so he waited a minute. The steps didn't get any louder, but after a while they stopped and the door opened, smoothly, and disappointingly creak-free.

The man framed in the doorway was a little shorter than Robbie, or at least he would have been, if he hadn't had an extravagantly domed bowler hat perched on top of his slicked-back hair. His nose was slightly too long, as if his mother had tweaked him by it too often as a baby, but otherwise he looked quite unremarkable. His suit was clean but cheap-looking, hanging in creases from his slight frame. His shoes were plain but well-worn, the toes scuffed then inexpertly repolished – a working man's shoes.

'Ah,' he said, touching his forefinger to his unsettlingly long nose. 'You must be Robbie. Come in, come in. We've been waiting for you.'

Robbie snuck a look at his watch – he was almost perfectly on time, a minute early, in fact – but then he realised that the man had already bustled along the short corridor and was holding another door open for him.

'Come along, come along. And shut that door behind you, won't you? The roads around here stink.'

'Thank you,' Robbie muttered, shuffling along the now darkened corridor. 'I wasn't sure I had the right place, but I assume I do – well I must, you know my name – only the man who left the message had a deeper voice, and I should say that I had to write the address down but there—'

He stopped when he entered the room. The man now stood against the far wall, his hands in his pockets. In front of him was a chair, and beside it were stacked five silver rings, one on top of the other, and a bundle of unlit wooden torches. The room was otherwise bare, although Robbie couldn't help noting several fresh-looking dents in the floorboards to one side.

'You're quite right,' said the man, and for a second Robbie couldn't fathom what he could possibly be right about. 'I am not he, not your employer, not the caller. Not *Sergei*. But I do run the circus for him, so I will be your first contact on all matters to do with *the act*. You may call me Mr Marcus. Everyone does. Now, if you'd like to change into your comfortable clothes – or not, it doesn't much bother me one way or the other – then kindly show me what you can do.'

Robbie felt two spots of heat rising to his cheeks as if he'd just been slapped.

'Oh. No, there's been a misunderstanding. I can't... I don't do it. This. I was hoping you could train me, or—'

'No problem at all. We don't expect any experience. We would have told you if we did. Just show me what you can do with these,' the man – Mr Marcus – wafted his hand in the direction of the chair and the juggling implements, 'and we can be getting on with things. Now, shall we?'

Robbie didn't feel right changing into his T-shirt, not with Mr Marcus watching, but he struggled out of his semi-smart black shoes and into his stained, torn fake Nikes.

'Like I say, I don't really know how—'

'Guess,' said Mr Marcus, twirling his hand in front of him in an unreadable gesture. 'Do your best and all that. Doesn't matter too much.'

Robbie took a breath, then stepped forward and lifted the rings. They were heavier than he'd expected, and he almost dropped them, just hanging onto one by the tips of his fingers. Once he was used to the weight he moved two of them across to his left hand, then he looked up again.

'Do I just...'

Mr Marcus did the wafting thing with his hand again.

Trying to keep his eyes on the rings, he tossed first one then another into the air, shifting his feet to give himself the best chance of catching them. One flew too far to the left, though, and clattered to the floor, while the other hit his hand, making him let go of the remaining rings with a yelp. There was a loud clang as they fell to the floorboards.

Nursing his fingers, Robbie looked up at the man.

'I'm sorry. Like I said… Should I try the others?'

Mr Marcus smiled and shook his head. 'No, let's not bother, shall we? I've seen all I need to see. If it's alright with you, we'd like you to start tomorrow.'

*

His first day with the circus was only slightly less confusing than the interview. When he arrived at the address Mr Marcus had given him, an area of open parkland on the edge of town, he found a ragged huddle of threadbare tents hastily thrown up on the grass. The guy ropes were crisscrossed in a chaotic web, and he had to tiptoe through them to reach the centre of the encampment. There stood a large marquee, hexagonal, its central peak propped up by a single pole. It may once have been striped green and red, but the colours had run and now it was mostly brown, with only occasional flashes of red showing through. The tent flaps were held open by what appeared to be a pair of hook-handled umbrellas stuck into the ground, and Mr Marcus was waiting for him inside.

'So good to see you Robbie,' he said, his hands again weaving patterns in the air before him. 'We're going to ease you in gently today, I think.'

Robbie nodded. Given his poor performance at the interview, he was still shocked to be there at all.

'This is yours,' Mr Marcus said, and from the floor he plucked a pointed metal stick.

Robbie stared at it. It looked like a sword. No, it *was* a sword. He hoped they weren't expecting him to eat it. He'd never really understood how sword-swallowers did their trick, and had always assumed it was an illusion of some kind. Without knowing the sleight of hand involved in the illusion, he wasn't terribly keen on eating it for real.

Mr Marcus clocked the worried expression on his face, but if he laughed it was only on the inside. As he spoke again he flipped the sword into the air, catching it deftly by the pointy end in his outstretched hand.

'For litter. Rubbish. Trash. You poke it, pick it up, then into a bag. Think you can manage that?'

And so Robbie spent his first day with the circus picking up candy wrappers, used tissues, the wrinkled rubber of burst balloons, and on one occasion a photo of Brad Pitt, torn from a magazine and smeared with what he hoped was French mustard. The job wasn't too bad at first, and he felt that he was starting to get the hang of it by lunchtime. He'd already filled three black rubbish sacks and the site was looking, if not exactly clean, then certainly in a more orderly state than when he'd arrived. Then the crowds came, queuing outside the marquee for twenty minutes to see the first performance of the day, and all his good work was undone. No matter how fast he worked, the constant drizzle of discarded plastic and soggy paper far outpaced him. By the time the interval between the shows came he was exhausted, demoralised and wading through an almost ankle-high drift of detritus.

He did his best to clear the swathes of trash before the day's second performance – the evening show – began, but he could barely see the grass when the queues started to form again. And as darkness fell, so people seemed to take that as a signal that they should drop their litter whenever and wherever they pleased. Come ten o'clock, as the final stragglers filed out of the marquee and staggered home, Robbie found himself at the centre of a miserable wasteland of crushed polystyrene and crisp packets. Even worse, he hadn't had the chance to take even a minute's break, meaning that, despite having been present for two of the circus's shows, he'd yet to see exactly what they did.

As he cast his eyes around at the filth, Mr Marcus swaggered out of the tent. Like Robbie, he looked at the garbage-strewn grass, then held his hand out for the sword.

'Excellent,' he said, his voice rising and falling with what Robbie confusingly suspected was excitement. 'Just as we thought. *Excellent*. Tomorrow we'll move you onto something more challenging, shall we?'

*

The next morning, Robbie made a little more effort than usual. He brushed his teeth, and spent several minutes plucking wayward eyebrow hairs with a pair of tweezers. If he was going to make his public debut, then he thought he should at least look presentable.

He needn't have bothered. Mr Marcus met him in the marquee tent again, only this time he handed him a long metal pole with a small open cage on one end. Robbie thought it looked like it should have graced a castle's battlements, fire roaring from the open end. Instead it was scratched and a little rusty, and it smelled faintly of Vaseline.

Robbie held it at arm's length while Mr Marcus gave him his marching orders for the day.

'We see great potential in you, Robbie – great, great potential. I have worked in Sergei's circus all my life and I know talent when I see it. So today, I have paired you with The Mighty Mungo. I can see you're excited. Mungo is the strongest man on three continents – which three, I forget –

and he draws quite a crowd. You will learn alongside him, be his right hand for the day. I have every faith in you.'

Robbie looked at the pole he'd been handed. It was surprisingly heavy, and the cage end kept dipping in the air, no matter how hard he tried to steady it. He wasn't sure what he was expected to do with it.

'Now, Mungo is waiting for you, so chop-chop. I'll see what you can do at showtime. I expect to be impressed.'

Mr Marcus held open a ragged flap at the back of the tent, and Robbie stooped to walk through, catching the pole on the canvas as he did so. Out the back of the marquee stood a rather squat but muscular man, his biceps the size of a grown man's head. He was stripped to the waist, and his torso was slick with a thick, yellow grease. His hair was cut in a ragged mullet at the back and he wore an incongruous stripe of glitter paint across both cheeks. He looked at least sixty years old.

'I am Mungo,' the man said, 'but you can call me Mighty Mungo. Now, we train.'

As it turned out, Robbie's contribution to the act didn't amount to much. Mungo spent the morning practising a routine with two large lead balls the size of cannonballs, steel handles welded to them so that he could juggle them, throw them, and generally make a show of tossing them up and then catching them again with a great, dramatic expulsion of air. As the grand finale of the act, Mungo would balance the pole upon his forehead and throw one of the balls up, catching it in the cage.

It was Robbie's job to pass him the pole.

To say that Robbie had hoped for more from his first circus outing would be an understatement, but he found that even this relatively simple task was fraught with pitfalls. The first time they attempted the handover he managed to clunk Mungo on the head with the pole, and while the strongman barely seemed to register the assault, it didn't exactly give the professional impression he'd been hoping for. The next, he handed him the pole upside-down and there was an awkward moment while Mungo set it right. Things hadn't improved much by the time they stopped for lunch.

A large crowd turned out for the afternoon show, and peering between the mouldy tent flaps Robbie could see that the marquee was jammed full. His palms were so sweaty that he kept wiping them on his inside-out T-shirt to keep them dry. The last thing he needed was for the pole to slip from his fingers.

It was the first time he'd had the opportunity to observe the other circus acts, and he gazed on in awe as Mistress Helga performed pirouettes on the tightrope, and a pair of twins known only as The Twins executed somersaults and other acts of derring-do on the trapeze. Of Sergei there was still no sign. There were a few moments when he found himself holding his breath along with the crowd, and he could see now why they swarmed here in their masses, day after day. There was something quite mesmerising about watching other people risk life and limb.

When The Mighty Mungo's turn came he leapt into the ring with his arms wide, displaying those infeasibly large biceps to full effect. Robbie snuck in behind him and did his best to merge into the shadows. He noticed a group of teenage lads in the front row pointing and laughing at Mungo's mullet, and he felt a surprising and overwhelming protectiveness towards the musclebound midget.

When his cue came, Robbie stepped forward into the spotlight and held out the pole. Mungo made a clumsy half-grab for it, his eyes fixed on the audience all the while, and when Robbie let go he didn't quite have hold of it. The pole fell to the compacted earth with a loud thud and

Mungo had to stoop to retrieve it, doing something with his eyes or his face that made the audience chuckle in complicity, although Robbie couldn't see what it was. He was too busy slinking back to hide in the shadows.

He figured he'd blown his chance, but when Mr Marcus cornered him after the performance his face was split by a wide grin.

'Excellent, young Robbie, excellent. I knew you had it in you.'

'I'm sorry I messed up, I think it was the lights or the—'

'Nonsense, you were perfect,' Mr Marcus said, his hands whirling. 'The crowd loved you. Let's do the same again tonight, shall we? Then we'll see about progressing you to something more challenging tomorrow.'

Robbie nodded and smiled, doing his best to hide his confusion.

*

And so it continued. When he was assigned to Mistress Helga, Robbie passed her the ballerina slippers in the wrong order, and she had to perform her act wearing them on the wrong feet; when he accompanied Bonzo the Clown into the ring he forgot to put the confetti into the bucket, and during his finale the funny man emptied exactly nothing over the heads of the audience members. Still, they laughed, even if they didn't know exactly why. He was a clown, ergo he must be funny.

It was after he'd been with the Circus du Sergei for almost three weeks that Robbie finally cornered Mr Marcus between the afternoon and evening shows. He had been rehearsing the speech in his head for several days, but now that his boss was staring at him down that overly long nose of his, the words didn't want to flow.

'I have a question, if that's okay. Please. I don't know... I was wondering...'

'You want to know what your place is here? Why we put up with your clumsiness – no, why we *adore* it – and what it is that you bring to our little circus act. Yes?'

Robbie simply nodded. It wasn't exactly what he'd been intending to say, but that was probably a good thing.

'The circus is not what people think,' Mr Marcus began. Robbie had the impression that this was a speech he'd given before. 'It is the glamour and the spotlight, yes, the amazing feats of strength and dexterity and balance. But more than anything else it is a show, and like any show it is meant to entertain its viewers, to tell them a story. Do you understand what I'm saying?'

Robbie nodded, although he didn't have a clue.

'The people who come to see us, they want to be thrilled, to be excited. And for that to happen, they have to be shown something dangerous. Does that make sense?'

Robbie nodded again, more vigorously this time. He could see that. From Mungo's cannonball-juggling to The Twins' aerial gymnastics, it all looked frightfully dangerous.

'Now, let me ask you,' Mr Marcus continued, 'which you find more exciting, more dangerous. A high-speed train racing through the countryside at sixty miles an hour? Or a homemade cart, constructed from old pram wheels and wooden pallets, rattling down a hillside at forty?'

Robbie barely paused. 'The cart.'

'Exactly. Slickness is not everything in our profession, young Robbie. Perfection does not make for great entertainment. We cultivate the imperfect because it allows people to believe in the danger, to be thrilled by it. If there were never any accidents, then what kind of show would we be?'

He wasn't sure if Mr Marcus expected an answer or not, so he nodded and smiled as if he understood.

'Excellent,' Mr Marcus said, rubbing his hands together. 'I'm glad we had this little chat.'

Robbie felt like he had a head full of questions, but he wasn't sure what any of them were. Instead he asked, 'Is there a Sergei? I mean, is he real? Will he be here soon?'

Mr Marcus smiled. 'Of course he's real. You see his name above our tent, don't you? He will come in good time, when everything is ready. Now, tomorrow I want to try you on something else. Something bigger. Tomorrow, you will be a star.'

*

Looking down from the top of the ladder, Robbie could see Mr Marcus waving at him. The bowler-hatted ringmaster was shouting something, and he had to strain to hear it.

'Grab it. Both hands! And stop looking down!'

He lifted his eyes again and saw the trapeze dangling in front of him. It was only two or three feet away, but at this height that gap felt like a chasm. They had a safety net of course. It had been his first question as soon as Mr Marcus had told him that one of The Twins was knocked out with the flu, and he'd received a chuckle in response. Yes, of course, he must practise with a net. They had all morning. By the afternoon show he would be an expert, he was sure of it. It was far, far easier than it looked.

Now, dangling halfway between ladder and trapeze, it felt anything but easy. Trying to keep his eyes from the ground – which, when he did glimpse it, seemed an infeasibly long way down – Robbie unpeeled his fingers from the ladder and grabbed at the trapeze bar with both hands.

'Excellent,' Mr Marcus shouted from below. 'Now jump! And swing!'

Fighting back an urge to be sick, Robbie closed his eyes and pushed off. As the trapeze swung back and forth he dared to open his eyelids a crack, watching as the marquee walls swung in and out of focus. His arms felt like they were being wrenched out of their sockets. His feet dangled uselessly beneath him, as if he were nothing more than a puppet. He couldn't imagine it looked terribly spectacular.

They attempted a few basic manoeuvres before Mr Marcus rang the gong for lunch, and as he climbed back down the ladder Robbie found that his arms and legs were shaking. When he reached the ground he could barely stand.

Mr Marcus clapped him on the back, almost sending him sprawling. 'See, that wasn't so bad? You looked wonderful up there. A natural.'

'My legs…'

'Don't worry about that. You'll get your sea legs after a while. You're just feeling the *rush*. The *adrenaline*. It will pass.'

When showtime rolled around, however, Robbie's legs were still shaking, and his arms felt like they were seizing up. This time he actually was sick, round the back of the marquee, where he was surprised to see two other small puddles of vomit joining his.

'Entertainment is a nervy business,' Mr Marcus assured him, handing him a thin paper napkin to wipe his lips. 'Let the crowd share your nerves. Let them feel the excitement.'

Climbing up the ladder, he could sense the ground growing more and more distant, the chatter of the crowd fading away. They were full again, for the sixteenth day in a row, and he could feel hundreds of eyes on him as he ascended into the dome of the tent. This was his time to shine. What had Mr Marcus told him? He would be a star.

He managed three swings on the trapeze before his left hand slipped, his fingers sweaty even through the chalk dust, and the pain in his right arm was so great that he managed to cling on for only a second. He didn't remember the fall – that passed by in a flash – but the sudden pain as he hit the ground was excruciating. His left foot hit the floor first, his leg crumpling beneath him like crushed cardboard, then his hip landed and he felt an almighty *crack* snap through him. He must have put his arms out in a vain attempt to steady himself, because they took the rest of the impact. He could feel his right forearm break, the ripping sensation as the bone tore through muscle and skin. The pain like pure white light. None of it was enough to keep his head from hitting the ground, and just before he passed out he caught a glimpse of his broken and mangled body, leaking blood into the dirt and the dust.

∗

Mr Marcus came to visit him in the hospital most mornings, although he never stayed late. The show had to go on, after all. Circus du Sergei had now sold out for a three-week run, the largest advance sales they'd ever experienced. The local paper had printed a story on the accident, and ever since they'd been playing to a full tent three times a day, an extra show squeezed into the early evening to help cope with demand. He knew all this because Mr Marcus told him. He did his best to nod, but the neck supports didn't really allow for any kind of movement, and even attempting it sent a spark of pain down his back that made his eyes water. Most times he managed a grunt and left it at that.

When his mum came to visit she brought him grapes, which of course he couldn't eat, and then she'd sit and wolf them down while staring at him, occasionally adjusting the covers over his pinned and plastered legs.

He noticed that she had a nice new handbag, and a cardigan that didn't have holes in the armpits. He assumed that Mr Marcus was to thank, although he wasn't able to ask.

Gradually, as the weeks rolled by, he came to accept his new role in life. It wasn't all bad. Everyone was always very nice to him, and he got to watch as much TV as he wanted, which was less entertaining than he would have expected, but still better than nothing. Occasionally he'd get an annoying tickle at the end of his nose, but otherwise he was pleasantly numb.

Then, one night, he had a dream. At least, he thought it was a dream, although given the quantities of self-service morphine pumping through him it might have been real, or something else altogether. He dreamed that the entire circus had come to visit him. Mr Marcus helped him up out of the bed, and The Mighty Mungo lifted him into a wheelchair. They wheeled him along the hospital corridors and out, out into the fresh air once again. He could feel it on his face, between the gap in his bandages, and he smelled what he thought was hot dogs. But when he looked around the world was different to how he remembered it. The buildings stood in ruins, the earth red and scorched. There were no people, but off in the distance he could hear a shouting and wailing, and his friends wheeled him towards it without him having to ask. And amidst the destruction they found a tent, the largest tent he had ever seen, and they pushed him inside and the people were there, everyone was there, the broken and the injured, the blind and the lame, all gathered around a rickety podium in the centre of the throng. Upon it stood a man with the legs of a goat, his skin black like leather, and when he saw Robbie he smiled and held out his hands. And Robbie knew without asking that this was Sergei, finally here in person, and everything would be just fine.

=ONLY THE BROKEN REMAIN=

During that first week, the noises waxed and waned. Some nights weren't too bad, while others offered only a couple of hours' rest before the rumpus began. The thudding against plaster, the high-pitched, childlike yelps. I considered going next door to complain, many times, but I couldn't imagine what I would say. My confidence had been broken by all that had happened, and I shrank away from the idea of confrontation. It was the most I could do to hurl a fist at the wall from time to time, adding my own thudding to the din.

On Tuesday I had my weekly call with James. The lab had insisted that I see him, when they were still invested in saving my career. Before I burned those bridges too. We'd met in person at first, at his featureless beige office, but now a weekly ten-minute call suited us both. There was no point in bailing out a ship that had already sunk.

'So how are you, Alison?'

'Okay. Fine, I guess.'

'Any relapses I should know about? Have you been drinking, or…'

'Nothing. I've been good.'

'And how are you sleeping?'

I knew he would register my pause. He was sharp like that. For a moment I considered lying, as if that might solve all my problems.

'Not well. My neighbour… it's always tough in a new place. She's just loud, is all. At night.'

'Have you spoken to her about it? If it's that bad? Or maybe some earplugs would help? You've come so far, we don't want you to slide back into old habits.'

'I haven't. Spoken to her, I mean. Or… the habits. I don't really feel comfortable with knocking on her door. Not yet. Sorry.'

We had spoken about my agoraphobia. James felt it was situational, a reaction to the extreme shocks and stresses of being sacked from my job. A knee-jerk against the loss of control. He was probably right but that didn't make it any easier. I could walk out the door anytime, but all I wanted to do was curl up on the couch and hide.

'You don't have to apologise. You've been through a lot. But if this problem is keeping you awake at night, you have to deal with it. Okay? Alison? You know that already, I think. Sooner or later, you have to face life again.'

I made the promises I needed to make, then he hung up with a reminder that I could call him at any hour, if I needed help. I didn't have the heart to tell him that I needed help all the time. As I made myself a cup of chamomile tea I noticed that someone had carved a crude height chart into the wood of the kitchen doorframe: a taller child, inching upwards; a slightly shorter sibling beneath them; then a series of scratches near the floor, the uppermost of them barely two feet from the ground. A dog, I assumed. The marks had been painted over at least once, the pools of emulsion failing to drown them out. Hard to imagine a family living here, in this stark two-up, two-down. It reminded me that my own family were no longer speaking to me, and I scratched my left palm until it was raw.

By the second week I had started to shout at the walls, begging for silence, but there was no indication that I'd been heard. If anything, the frequency and intensity of the noises increased. I heard them during the day sometimes. No matter how high I turned the volume on the TV they were still there. It made it worse, somehow, that I couldn't hear what she was saying. I tried to distract myself with the unpacking, piling books against the walls to try and muffle the noise. I pushed the few remaining boxes into the small cupboard beneath the stairs, closing the door on them. There was a rusted bolt at the top which I pulled across for good measure.

The combination of withdrawal and sleeplessness had stretched me thin, until I felt that something must snap. I had red, eczema-like patches on both hands where I'd clawed at them. Finally I pulled on my waterproof and stepped out into the rain.

From the pavement the next-door tenement looked dead, its windows dark and filmed with dirt. As I walked up her path, tugging at my hood to keep the rain from my eyes, I could see thick, yellowed curtains hanging in the windows. The door was white and windowless, with no knocker or bell to be seen. I paused with my hand raised, knuckles pointing forward. A light tap at first, becoming louder as my frustration got the better of me. Nothing. Louder this time, using the side of my fist too: *tap-tap-tap, thud thud, tap-tap.* Step back. No chink of light through the curtains, no sign of movement. I knew she was in there. The silence felt like a taunt.

Then I remembered that the properties all had back entrances, and I splashed through the puddles to the path that led down the side of my house. The estate agent had tried to make a feature of it, this access route through the back gardens. Perfect for the amateur gardener, he'd said. Then he'd looked at me, and turned away.

The path was unlit, but I found her gate easily enough. The wood was so damp that I feared it might crumble and collapse beneath my hand like soggy cardboard, but it swung open when I pushed. The garden was dark and untended, brambles running riot along either fence, what might once have been a lawn lost in a knee-high profusion of grass and weeds. There was still a path of sorts, and I could wade through the plant growth, my jeans sticking to my legs as the rainwater seeped in. Once I reached the back of the house I was able to stand on tiptoe and peer in through the window to the kitchen, my hands clasped to my face. It was too dark to see clearly. Then I remembered my phone and, activating the flashlight function, I lifted it to the glass.

Nothing. I could see into the room well enough, but there was nothing there. No furniture, no ornaments. A rusted sink streaked with black and grey. An empty light fitting. Nothing more than a thick layer of dust on tired linoleum, forming a furred carpet that stretched undisturbed into the empty room beyond.

There was no one living there. There was no neighbour. It occurred to me for the first time that I might be going mad.

I sat shivering under a towel in my living room for the rest of the evening, trying to make sense of the noises I could hear. They came from next door, of that I had no doubt. The only other possibility was that they originated from within the wall itself, and I wasn't prepared to accept that explanation. Neither were they a figment of my imagination. I'd had issues recently, true, but I still knew reality from fiction. As I thought that, there was a new thud and a crackle of laughter from the wall, as if she was mocking me. *Is this what madness feels like?* I thought. *Am I too far gone to even know?*

I called James a little after ten, on the private mobile number he'd given me. The one for emergencies. I could hear the sleep in his voice when he answered, a brief snap of annoyance that was quickly smothered. His professional tone re-established itself.

'Is everything okay, Alison? Are you having a relapse?'

'No. And no.'

'What is it then? It's late...'

'How do you know if you're going mad? I mean, if you're crazy, you wouldn't know it, would you? So how do you know?'

He snorted, a failed attempt to suppress a laugh.

'If you're asking that question, then you're probably still sane. In my experience, the people with serious problems are buried too deep in them to even acknowledge their existence. But what's brought this on? Is everything okay?'

No, I wanted to say. No, it's not. My neighbour doesn't exist. I've been hearing phantom noises in the walls. I'm cold, and wet to the skin, and I can still hear her laughing. Her non-existent fists thudding against the plaster. So no, I'm not okay.

'Its fine,' I said. 'It's all fine, I'm sure.'

'Good. Well, maybe call me tomorrow, okay? And stay away from the alcohol tonight, and the pills. They only make it worse. We'll talk in the morning.'

He hung up.

It was as I walked into the hallway, draping the damp towel across the radiator to dry, that I noticed the door to the cupboard under the stairs. It hadn't occurred to me before, but it made no sense that there should be a bolt on it, did it? Bolts were intended not just to keep doors closed, but to keep someone from opening them. But if the bolt was on this side, then who was the bolt intended for? Who – or what – was on the inside trying to get out?

I stared at it for several minutes before I found the courage to kneel and force the bolt across. It was stiff, but after a twist or two it slid out of the latch. I could feel my hands shaking as I pulled the door open and started to drag out the boxes I'd stored inside. Once they were piled up behind me I took out my phone again, holding its flashlight tentatively into the cupboard space, half expecting something to leap out and grab me. There were cobwebs in the corners, and a littering of dead insects on the floorboards, but no other signs of life. The noise from next door had become frenzied. Without thinking, I crawled into the empty space. It felt somehow peaceful in there, silent. Reaching for the door, I found a small handle only a few inches from the ground, as if someone had always intended for me to hide inside.

Then I smelled it. As I shuffled closer to the back wall the stench overtook me: a damp mustiness, like compost or mould, cut with something like sweat, or urine, sharp and threatening. I gagged, my pulse racing. Without thinking what I was doing, I scuttled back out of the door, shutting it behind me. My hand found the bolt and drew it across.

It took two cups of tea to calm the jitters, another before I could consider what I wanted to do. The noises had quietened next door, although they were still there, muted. As if whatever was making them had moved further away. I considered sleeping on it, but sleep felt unfeasible. A little after midnight I armed myself with a hammer and a torch, and, with trembling fingers, reopened the door.

It was easy enough to prise up the floorboards. They were old and crumbling in places, the nails sliding free without resistance. When the stink became too strong I took my shirt off and wrapped it around my face, tying the sleeves at the back. It didn't negate it entirely, but it helped. Beneath the boards was a network of pipes, tarnished and greening around the joints; beneath them, nothing but fine, gritty dirt. The back corner, where the smell was strongest, was free of pipework. Propping the torch against the wall, I set to work with my hands. My palms were still sore, and I could feel the skin splitting as I dug, but I ignored the pain. The pile of displaced dirt was streaked in places with my blood.

I found her about six inches down, where the dirt started to turn to clay, moist and slimy to the touch. Her head crowned first, the smooth white dome of her skull blooming from the soil. With my fingers I dug around her, clearing the way. Finally I was able to slide my fingers underneath her and lift her out of the hole.

She had been wrapped in course cloth of some kind, but it had mostly rotted away, only a few rags left clinging on. I unwrapped her from her crude swaddling on the hallway floor. Bones, only bones remained. Her head as large as an infant of three or four, but distorted, the top bulging outwards; her body twisted back, her neck unnaturally long. The arms and hands looked strange, and it took me a moment to realise that they were indistinguishable from her legs, the angles of the elbows all wrong, the hands long and bent back, like feet.

I remembered the height chart on the kitchen doorframe. The lowest notches, that I had assumed belonged to a pet. Not a dog, then. She must have lived for a few years at least, for the marks to have been made. The terrible secret. A family's shame.

I looked at the bolt on the cupboard door again. At the handle by the floor. The noises next door became sadder, somehow, like a whimper. When I couldn't stand it anymore I looked away.

I'd read enough about hauntings to know what I had to do. She wasn't at peace, that much was clear. She was still locked away in that cupboard, a prisoner in her family's home. I knew how that felt, to exist within the four walls of a shrunken world. To be the shame your parents refused to speak of. I bundled her inside the towel from the radiator, taking care to wrap her tight. Clutching her to my chest, the torch wedged under my arm, I carried her out into the garden.

It took me two hours to dig the hole beneath the bay tree. By the time I finished the sun was just starting to blush on the horizon, and the rain had eased off. Wet and tired, I lowered her into the ground. There should have been some words I could say, something to put her at peace, but my background was never a religious one. Maybe if it had been I would have found the strength to fight my own demons. Maybe it didn't make any difference at all.

When she was covered, the ground patted down into a gentle mound, I fashioned a crude cross from two sticks and pushed it into the dirt. That would have to be enough. She was out of the house at last.

Once back indoors I was too wired to sleep, so I made myself a cup of tea and ran a hot bath. While it ran I pushed the boards back into the cupboard, stacked my boxes inside. I didn't bother with the bolt. The bath did its job, easing away the tension, the ache from the digging, the cold that had seeped into my legs. Several times I jerked awake, my head almost sagging into the water. After the fourth time I got out and dried myself, tumbling into bed. I slept until the evening.

The funny thing is, it didn't work. Not quite. I still hear her sometimes, scuttling behind the walls, yelping in the night. Not as often as before, but she's there. I guess I didn't know as much about hauntings as I thought. But it's easier to deal with, somehow. Now that I know her. Now that I know her pain. When she wakes me in the middle of the night, with a thump against the wall, I put my hand out and rest it against the plaster. I whisper lullabies, calm her back to sleep. Sometimes she takes longer than others, but she knows I'm here now. She knows I'm here for her. I can live with that.

FEATHER AND TWINE

He discovered the bird in the doorway as he opened the shutters for the day. A European starling, its body speckled with white, its head fuzzed brown in winter plumage. Its neck was broken, one of its wings twisted back. Feathers splayed. Looking at the door, there was a new crack in the glass.

Brandon took it in his hands, cradling it gently between his palms. With a swift tug, he pulled the broken wing back into place. He could hear it snap. Bustling inside, he carried it through to the workshop. The freezer was almost full, but he found some space at the back, among the sparrows, nestled next to the muscular bulk of a red-tailed hawk. Closing the door his hands were tingling and numb.

Returning to the front, he turned on the neon sign to say that he was open. Then he shut the door against the winter winds and started work.

*

On the rare occasions when customers engaged him in conversation, they were surprised to find that Brandon was softly-spoken but articulate, intelligent and well-educated. His training as an architect had never completely been forgotten, and from time to time he would enjoy a discussion on the way the Bloomberg Tower reflected the late-afternoon light, or the Gothic splendour of the Radiator Building. Most times, though, he would keep to himself, his eyes on the table, his mutterings brief and to the point. He had work to do. There was no space for distractions.

Mostly they brought their pets to him, expecting miracles. Chihuahuas, chinchillas, mastiff hounds. Occasionally they'd had the forethought to freeze them, but often they were recently dead, not quite decomposing, their bodies rigid with the shock of mortality. Sometimes they had been mauled by another animal, their skin torn, their fur stained. He charged extra for those. One woman brought her cat to him after it had been run over by a truck – her, he turned away.

The birds were his specialty, though. Of the fourteen qualified taxidermists in New York, he was the only one who could construct a realistic frame for a lovebird, or set a parrot with its beak wide open, mid-squawk. He had a reputation amongst those in the know. The Bird Man, they called him; Feather-Boy, if they were older. He did nothing to discourage them.

There were still days when his father would call, pretending to ask about the business, actually trying to persuade him to return to his studies. Architecture was a boom industry, didn't he know? The potential for a six-figure salary was hard to ignore. Didn't he want to be successful? Didn't he want to make the best possible use of his talents?

Brandon remained silent for most of the conversations, sometimes grunting or whispering a reply. He never gave his father false hope, and he never wavered. He had his shop. He had his work. That was enough for him.

Neither of them mentioned the incident on the subway, or the way he'd suddenly dropped out of school. It sat behind every conversation like a stain.

*

Brandon sat on his stool at the back of the shop and arranged his tools in front of him. Twigs and twine, needle and thread. Salt, oil, Borax. Five knives of differing sizes, all the way down to the delicate dentistry scalpel he'd found online. All immaculately cleaned, all impressively sharp.

Today's job was a house cat, simple enough and unlikely to challenge him. It had died of a tumour, the bulge of it swelling sickeningly smooth beneath its ear, like a second head trying to burst through the skin. It would have to be removed, the skin stitched expertly behind it. He relished the work. He knew he could do it easily, the diseased tissue disappearing as if it had never existed. If that made him godlike, he didn't feel much like a god.

The birds were what he lived for. Their delicate frames held so much scope for failure, working with them was a tightrope walk that he relished and feared. Whenever someone brought in a parakeet or a cockatoo he could feel his pulse quicken, in anticipation of the work to come. They paid well, too. Not quite six figures, but the shop did okay. It was remarkable what people would pay to see their loved ones stuffed and mounted.

The wild birds he kept for himself. They filled the freezer, crammed in alongside the cats and dogs. After the door closed, after the shutters went down, his real work began.

*

It was a hot summer's day when it happened. He can remember that much. He still dreams about it sometimes, the emotions resurfacing like a drowned body, bloated and pale. Those nights he wakes feeling sick, his body shimmering with tiny convulsions, his head pounding. Sometimes he still believes he can see it for a moment, silhouetted against the bare wall, looming in the shadows.

He'd been late for lunch with his father, one of those sporadic meals he was expected to attend where he would have to give updates on his studies, estimations of his grades. He never had anything new to say, but that didn't seem to discourage the old man. He had made it clear that they were funding his studies in the expectation that he would care for them through their twilight years. He was an investment, of time and money. They expected their dividends.

The decision to take the subway was a last minute one. He never liked the cramped conditions, the metallic smell of the rails – the crowds were worse in summer, too. But he couldn't bear the recrimination if he turned up thirty minutes late again, the barbed comments, the disappointed looks. It was easier to bear the discomfort.

The 6 train was crowded, tourists chattering and smiling for selfies amidst the usual, dour faces of the downtowners. He wished he had thought to take off his blazer. Crammed into the car, his arms pressed to his sides, he was stuck with it as surely as if he'd been tied into a straitjacket. He could feel the trails of sweat worming their way down his back, the droplets forming on his forehead, growing slowly, threatening to fall. His breath was short and his fingertips tingled. He reminded himself to breathe.

He had been heading up to Union Square, but he never got that far. It happened not long after they'd pulled away from Brooklyn Bridge-City

Hall, the car rattling around them, the darkness outside accelerating. He was trying to concentrate on his breathing, on the hand clutching the rail. Ignoring the cold stickiness of his body, the waves of heat that fell over him as the air shifted and changed. He stared out of the window, his eyes focusing on nothing, allowing the blackness beyond the glass to absorb him.

Then he saw it. It was there one second and gone the next, but he was in no doubt that it was real. The image had imprinted itself upon him, a single frame of exposure in the dark room of the train. A face. A creature. A *thing*.

The paramedics told him later that he'd passed out, had suffered some kind of seizure. It had frightened the other people in the car, so they'd said. Convulsions, frothing at the mouth. They thought it might be epilepsy, but he had no history of it, and later the tests showed nothing either. He'd blacked out and lost almost twenty minutes of his life. There was a tender red lump on the back of his head where he'd hit the floor.

He told them what he saw, as they monitored his blood pressure and his heart rate, his temperature and his pupil dilation. Something not quite like a man, too big to be human; two arms, two legs, but still not one of us. Eight feet tall, he'd guess. Maybe nine. Naked, its body well-muscled but somehow hazy, as if covered in a fine layer of fur. Two enormous wings unfurling from its back, each one long enough to envelop a man, the feathers tousled by the wind in the tunnel, in constant motion as it flew alongside them. Its face large but kind, questioning.

One hand reaching out to take his.

*

Brandon locked up a little after six. The cat was almost finished, just a few final touches to attend to tomorrow. There had been no new business that day, but that wasn't unusual. Most days he would sit at his bench alone, immersed in the work. Sometimes it was a shock to see another human face.

Although work was finished for the day he didn't clear away his tools. He still had much to do, so much to achieve. He had been chipping away at it for months now but he felt he was almost there, almost at the point where he could unveil his masterpiece to the world. The toil had been long and hard. He knew it would be worth it.

Five birds lay in a line on the bench, arranged from the smallest to the largest. A sparrow, starlings, the dirty grey of a rock pigeon. They had defrosted slowly, a single layer of paper beneath them soaking up the moisture. One of the starlings he had found in the park on a rare expedition out into the city, but the others had all come to him, their bodies appearing on his doorstep. Some days there would be two or three, like an offering. He suspected that the glass confused them, with its reflections of clear blue sky, its illusion of freedom. Many had broken necks, but that didn't trouble him. It was the feathers he wanted.

The process of detaching the wings was simple enough, but he took his time. He had to make sure that they remained intact. In the early days he had broken a bone here and there in his frantic rush to prepare them, and the end results had to be thrown out, the process started all over again. He had learned to be patient.

Picking up a scalpel he started making the incisions, breaking the surface of the skin, exposing the fine, brittle bones. This part was easy now, he had practiced it over and over. Detaching the wing itself was where the damage could be done. He finished the incisions on all five birds before he began to delicately bend the joints, severing the sinews with a fine blade as the wings came away. He worked slowly and methodically, disassembling them one by one. When he had finished, there were ten wings lined up in front of him; two lines, five to the left, five to the right.

The scalpels and knives went into the tub to be sterilised, then he gently lifted each wing onto a tray. The twine and thread he took with him, along with the tray, heading up the stairs to his personal quarters. Beyond his bedroom, beyond the cramped kitchenette, lay his other workshop.

*

He hadn't abandoned his studies immediately. He had persevered for several months, trying to ignore the headaches, the nausea that swelled within him unexpectedly as he went about his day. He tried telling his father what he had seen, but it never came out right. He stumbled over his words, got confused trying to describe the creature that had burned itself onto his mind. He could tell that the old man didn't believe any of it. Why should he? He barely knew what it was himself, or what it meant. He had no words to describe the bird-thing living under the city streets; the angel, as he thought of it. No rational reason for it being there, no knowledge of what had driven something born to fly so far beneath the ground. He vaguely recalled rumours of a disused subway station around there, but that explained nothing, illuminated nothing. He knew how he must look.

He made the decision a couple of weeks before he officially quit. It seemed so obvious, the only thing to do. Sitting outside the college one day, his head pounding, his stomach twisted into knots, he watched a small, brown bird hopping among some crumbs beneath the trashcan. It watched him from the corner of its eye, its body in constant motion as it hopped and looked, hopped and pecked, looked and ate. He didn't move, simply sat there, immersed in the bird's actions. When it flew away, finally, the flutter of its wings sent a shudder through his body, a tremor that he could feel in every muscle, every tendon. He saw the face smiling at him through the window again, just for a second; the hand held out, waiting.

He didn't go to any lessons after that. By the time they sent a letter asking why he wasn't attending classes, he had already put in an offer on the vacant property. His architecture books had been traded in for a volume on taxidermy. He had enrolled in the home study course online.

The disappointment in his father's voice when he told him was abundantly clear, but it was also underlined with confusion. Why was he doing this? How could he throw away everything that he – they – had worked for?

He couldn't explain. Didn't try to. It was enough that it made sense to him. And the memories started coming as soon as he began work on the birds, brushing his hands across their feathers, feeling for the bone structure beneath. Sometimes as dreams, sometimes during the day, in the subdued, brown light of his workspace. Simply a memory of the size of the thing, or its presence outside the subway car. Sometimes its face, up close to the glass, familiar and yet otherworldly, bestial and yet infinitely wise. Sometimes nothing more than the rush of its wings in the stale air.

He started the project not long after. There were false beginnings, but not too many. He was a quick study. The pictures in his mind started to take on a physical form.

*

Brandon stood for a moment in the attic doorway before switching on the light. He could smell it in the room, musty and dry, but potent too, like an animal that has been caged for too long.

Once light bathed the room he moved forward, the tray held before him. It had taken him almost a month to construct the frame, a structure of bamboo canes and twine mostly, dwindling down to sticks and string at the extremities. He had bought a mannequin from a fire sale to mount it on, the head blackened and charred on one side, one arm missing. It didn't matter. The body was simply a stand to hang it from, a place to rest it while he worked. The harness he had stitched from leather straps, old buckles, held together by catgut. The mannequin wore it like a parachute.

It didn't take him long to add the wings to the frame. He had done this many times before, maybe hundreds. He had lost count. When he stepped back he could see that his work was almost finished. Maybe one more day, maybe two. No more than six or seven birds. He had enough to finish it.

He checked the glue before he left, tested its strength. Everything held. At the top of the stairs he stumbled, caught his breath, his legs feeling light and faint beneath him. For a second there he felt as if he was floating, suspended in the air. He smiled as he took the steps carefully, one at a time, down to his bedroom below.

*

He closed up early that night. Secured all the locks, turned off the neon light. It was still not quite five o'clock, and the light outside was only just waning. The dirty street was washed in pale gold.

The tools were still arrayed on his worktop, but for once he didn't bother to put them away. It didn't seem necessary anymore. They could stay there, where people would find them. So they could see what he had done.

As he walked up the stairs he felt his body growing lighter, as if he was already ascending into the clouds. There was a dull throb behind his eyes but he welcomed it, allowing it to spread through him, giving a rhythm to his actions. He knew now that he had been touched by something that day – an angel, a visitor, or perhaps something older, something that had always been there, down in the tunnels. It didn't matter that he couldn't give it a name. It only mattered that he recognised what it needed, and that he was coming. He was ready.

It took him a few minutes to unstrap the harness from the mannequin. He knew he had to be careful, that nothing could be allowed to break, not now. He was tempted to strap it onto himself immediately, but he had learned the right way to do things, and the wrong. He carried it carefully to the top of the stairs, watching out for the door frame. From there, he was able to open the window and climb onto the fire escape. The harness he manoeuvred through the window behind him, the seven-foot wings attached to either side brushing the wood as they passed. When it was outside, intact, he shrugged it onto his back. It was shockingly light, barely there at all. Once he had tightened all the buckles he was able to stand tall, a man become a bird, a man become an angel.

He swung one leg over the railing, then the other, his weight balanced on the narrow strip of metal. Looking up, he could see the city laid out in front of him, the shadows long and deep as the sun dipped into the west, the man-made structures rising from the land like failed monuments.

Closing his eyes, he recalled the rush of the train, the clatter, the shuddering. He remembered that moment, standing there, the heat wrapped around him, as his angel appeared from the darkness and held out its hand. He was being chosen. He knew that. The thing in the tunnels had chosen him, and he had responded.

When he opened his eyes again the city was almost dark, the wind blowing cold into his face. Then, from the rooftops, from the parks, from the trees, there arose a twittering and a chattering, the song of thousands of birds, millions, their beaks open in a call to the air. And Brandon watched as they rose and swirled around him, a scything flock of tiny angels, lifting him away he knew not where.

=MIRIAM IS NOT AT HER DESK=

Miriam stumbles as she steps off the plane. Someone guides her hand to the rail that runs the length of the boarding tunnel, and as she steadies herself she realises she's left her sunglasses in Singapore. She'll have to buy some. The sunlight here is fiercer; she can feel it burning its way through her at a molecular level, illuminating places she'd rather leave in the dark.

It's easy enough to find a pair of glasses, but they're all surfer wraparounds, plasticky and cheap. Maybe everybody loses their glasses here. She settles on the plainest pair she can find, although even these sit at odds with her tailor-made twin-set. As she waits for her luggage she peers through the blue-grey lenses at a mural on the wall of the airport lounge. She should enjoy the geometry, the accumulation of thousands of circles of pure colour, but this one confuses her. The shapes feel random, unformed, and she struggles to work out what it means. She tries defocusing her eyes, as if it's a Magic Eye picture. It doesn't help. She feels unbalanced, and slightly sick.

On Malcolm's advice, she saw a doctor about the dizzy spells last time she was in London. They did some scans. Whole afternoons wasted sitting in papery gowns, staring at grey walls beyond the revolving machines. They found nothing, of course. The doctor said it was down to anxiety, the high-stress life she led. He gave her some pills. She has left those in the hotel in Singapore too. This time it wasn't accidental.

Her luggage takes forever to come, a single hard-shell wheelie case in chocolate brown. Opposite her stands a family of four, still waiting for their baggage. They are starting to look unsettled, slowly acknowledging that bad news is on its way. She looks at their little girl, something pink and fluffy clutched to her chest, daring the customs officials to tear it away from her. She turns her back on them and wheels her case towards the taxi rank.

*

Her hotel spreads its legs across half a block of the Central Business District. Her room is on the twentieth floor. She can see the harbour from the window, one end of the bridge where it touches down in The Rocks. It reminds her of a rainbow, and she wonders where the crock of gold lies. Not here, that seems certain. Maybe in a Swiss bank account. An offshore account in the Caymans.

The bathroom is clean and modern, well stocked with tiny shampoos, moisturisers, conditioners. There's even a tiny pumice stone, the size of a baby mouse. She runs a bath and pours in something green, allowing herself to wallow in the sharp, herbal scent. Eucalyptus, she thinks. Maybe a hint of rosemary. When she steps out of the water her vision swims for a moment and she has to sit down on the toilet seat to regain her balance. She blames the heat this time, the steam. It occurs to her that she hasn't had a bath in her own house for almost a month. It's always hard to judge a bath when you're away from home.

She sits on the bed in her complimentary bathrobe and slippers, waiting for the Wi-Fi to connect. There's a framed picture on the wall opposite the bed, a barren canyon among red rocks, a hazy white sky looming above them. She isn't sure if it's a photo or a painting. Either way, it makes her skin itch. All the moisture from the bath sucked away by that alien dust. She turns back to the screen and waits for the hourglass to flip.

Once the Internet pings to life she logs into her bank accounts, checks the figures. It's all there. No one has taken it away. It was intended to soothe her mind, but she finds that the sight of it stokes her anxiety again. Her throat closes up, puckering shut. There's a tightness in her chest, as if she has just swallowed something far too large and it's stuck there, rotting. It's a lot of money. Almost too much to be real.

Her finger jabs the power button, the screen blinks to black. She knows she won't sleep now, so she swings her legs over the edge of the bed, stares at the chocolate-brown case. Maybe she should go out.

*

She has always preferred Sydney at night. Away from the glare of sun, the city blooms; the streets flow cool and inviting, the bars stand proud, swathed in lights. Miriam wanders with the other moths, flitting from bar to bar, killing time. As she reaches Circular Quay a dinner cruise is preparing to depart. She pays the ridiculous last-minute ticket fee and steps onto the water. The man who sells her the ticket looks at her as if she's mad. It's a fair assessment, in her opinion. It would explain a lot.

While couples and business parties grin into the night breeze, she sits indoors, forcing herself to sip at an overpriced martini. She knows she could get very drunk tonight, and that would be a bad idea. Even standing outside feels risky. The city lights shimmer on the surface of the water, a shoal of miraculous fishes making patterns for her entertainment. It would be easy to topple over the rail, find yourself down there with them, in the cold of the harbour. She could blame it on the fainting spells, if she wanted to. Everyone would, when they dragged her out. Maybe not once they'd checked her finances, though. Maybe not then.

The food is passable, better than she expected, although the Oysters Kilpatrick repeat on her for the rest of the night. She's glad to disappear into the tangle of bodies as they disembark at the quay, caught up for a moment in their conversations, their laughter. She hears a London accent somewhere and it reminds her of home. Malcolm. She hasn't quite said it to herself until now, but there's no going back. There's a return ticket somewhere in her case. She reminds herself to throw it away when she gets back to the room. Tear it into pieces, just to make sure.

She takes her time strolling back to the hotel. The air is cool now, a welcome balm before tomorrow's oven-like heat. There are goosepimples on her arms but she doesn't cover them. Her skin prickles with life. It's easy to forget sometimes that she hasn't disappeared altogether.

As she turns the corner by the hotel she spots something bundled in a shop doorway. It looks false, somehow, oversized clothes stuffed with newspaper and straw, a face barely scrawled on crumpled brown paper. A penny for the guy, mister. But then it moves, shifting its weight as it sleeps, and she can see the face clearly. An Aboriginal man, his skin creased like crepe paper, one deep furrow slicing through his brow like a scar. She's too far away to smell him, but she still forms the impression that he reeks. Of sweat, of booze. She can smell the eucalyptus on her own skin, and her mind jumps back to the laptop again, all those figures on the screen. If he had only a fraction of what she has now, it would change his world forever. It occurs to her that she should just give it to him. All of it, every penny.

It isn't hers to give, but maybe something good could come out of this. Maybe two wrongs really could make a right.

All she finds in her pockets are a few sales receipts and the pair of sunglasses she bought at the airport. Unfolding the arms, she props them against his paper cup, a surprise for when he wakes.

She rubs a little heat into her arms and keeps walking.

*

Lacking anything better to do, Miriam spends the next day drifting through the shopping malls. They are cool at least, and out of the sun. From time to time she has to step outside, to hail a taxi, to cross the street. Even those few minutes are too much for her. At the taxi rank she has another dizzy spell, and the driver eyes her with suspicion, pausing a moment before opening the door. It's true that she feels as if she might be sick, but it soon passes. She wonders again if the doctor might have got it wrong. It would make so much more sense if it were a tumour, a violent mass encroaching on her brain. All of this would be understandable, then. A story that encourages pity, rather than retribution.

At Bondi Junction she buys some better sunglasses, a stylish pair of Ray-Bans that suit her face. Her other purchases are slight: a romance novel, an electric toothbrush, some painkillers when a headache threatens to overtake her. She buys a small box of PG Tips when she spots it, for an extortionate price. It reminds her of home, the bold red and green lettering, the deep blue of the sky. As she leaves the mall she drops it into a rubbish bin.

Back in the hotel, she stops at the bar for a drink. It's mid-afternoon. The place is almost deserted. Two men in suits at a table in the corner, an elderly couple deep in discussion with the concierge. The barman smiles when she orders a dry martini, her co-conspirator in throwing caution to the wind.

'Extra olive with that? They're good.'

Miriam wonders briefly if he's flirting with her. He's young enough to be her son, if she had one. There's only Malcolm in her life, though, and even he has been shrugged aside now. She feels old.

'Yes please. Make it strong, will you?'

There's the briefest of nods, then he turns his back on her, reaching for a bottle on the shelf. He's not that attractive, not really, but his back is muscular, his body well-defined in that way she's noticed among the surfing crowd. *Where were you when I was younger?* she thinks, sipping the drink he sets in front of her. *Where did all those years go?*

'Are you here on business? Or pleasure?'

The question catches her off-guard. Which is it? This doesn't feel much like pleasure, but there's no going back to her job either. If there were an option for running away, she would take it. Press the button that says 'disappear here'. For the briefest moment she considers confessing everything to him. Isn't that what barmen are for? Her dissatisfaction with the life she has built, the meaninglessness of these things she gathers around her, all these particles of junk in her orbit. It might feel good to unburden herself at last. It might start to make sense.

'Business, I'm afraid. Just taking an extra day or two. To unwind.'

He smiles. 'Best place in the world to do it. Maybe I'll see you down the beach sometime. Watch your skin, though. You Poms burn up over here.'

Then he's gone, rearranging glasses at the other end of the bar. She watches him as she finishes her drink, the way he casually joins the conversation between the two suited gentlemen, the ease with which he carries himself. She can't remember a time when she was ever that at home in her body. She twists the wedding band on her finger and wonders why it's still there.

In the lift she finds it hard to breathe and she has to sit on the floor. When the doors open there's a maid standing there, confusion on her face. She picks herself up and strides as confidently as she can to her door. Don't look back. Once the door is closed, she lies on the bed until the moment passes.

*

The last time she saw Malcolm was three weeks ago, at the end of November. He had a conference in the city, was staying at their house in Sevenoaks. She was between business trips, passing through on her way to Dubai. Their paths crossed for two days. She found it hard to look him in the eye, knowing what she had done. The money was in her accounts by then – the new, private accounts, not their shared assets. She was already pulling away and his presence came as a shock. She felt certain he could see the guilt etched on her face.

It was over breakfast on the second day that he asked her. His lean, stringy body had spooned her during the night, a forgotten warmth at her back. She hadn't responded as he'd wrapped his arms about her. She had pretended she was still asleep.

'Do you ever wish we'd done this differently? Us, I mean? Would it have been different if we'd had kids?'

She'd kept stirring her cereal around the bowl, tiny islands in a sea of milk.

'Do you?'

There was that snort he made when he was half laughing, half serious, and she looked up. She thought, just for a second, that she saw a sadness there, a loss that resonated with her own.

'Maybe. Sometimes. I don't know, to be honest. They look like an awful lot of work. We couldn't have been where we are today.'

Yes, Miriam thought. We wouldn't have been where we are today.

Maybe that's the point.

*

It's not until Thursday night that she can bring herself to connect the laptop again. Nestled among the usual emails is one from Alan, her boss. She delays opening it, wastes several minutes reading and deleting updates from the Royal Society of Accountants, offers of double points from Boots. Finally, she clicks.

It's shorter than she expected. The tone is confused rather than accusatory. He writes that he's tried to contact her but her phone is off. He says they've noticed 'discrepancies'. He's at an artist meeting in New York until the end of the week, but she can call him or text him any time. He hopes that everything is okay.

Miriam stares at it for several minutes, trying to read between the lines. They have found that the money is missing, then. She knew they would, eventually, but still it feels shocking. It leaves her raw, exposed. She has some silly idea that the police might be able to hijack her laptop, that they could trace her here, peer out at her through the treacherous eye of her webcam. Hurriedly, she turns the laptop off and pulls the plug. She can feel her heart thumping in her chest.

When she tries to sleep, she ends up lying in bed for an hour, wide awake, her eyes fixed on the picture of the desert opposite. It scares her still, with its unrelenting heat, its parched red dust, but there's an attraction, too, mingling with the fear. It's the kind of place someone might vanish completely. No Wi-Fi, no webcams, no roads. As her eyelids droop she feels like she's staring at another planet.

*

Exiting the lift she looks for the barman again, but he isn't there. Must be his day off. Miriam imagines him out in the surf, his face misted with sea-spray, his body tensed as he waits for a wave. In reality, he's probably propping up another bar somewhere, or slouched at home on the couch. Whatever it is that off-duty barmen do.

Instead, she asks the concierge if he can recommend a restaurant. He replies with a grunt and a noncommittal shrug. She doesn't like him. A certain type of surly male, wrapped up in his ape-like ego. When she presses him he says that the tapas bar around the corner is popular.

'But is it any good?'

That grunt again. It sets her teeth on edge.

'I've not eaten there myself but people seem to like it. You'll just about catch happy hour. If you're lucky.'

She seethes at the implication that she's a happy hour kind of person, but he's right – when she gets there it does look busy, and the garlicky smells are encouraging. They give her a table at the rear, offering only a view of the kitchen doors and a cork sculpture of a bull mounted on the wall. They apologise for the scenery, but it doesn't bother her. Back here she's in hiding.

The chorizo is rich, if a little oily, but the bread is good and the salad looks crisp and generous. It's as she tucks into a forkful of *patatas bravas* that she crunches down on something gritty in the dish. Residual dirt on the potato skins, she assumes. But then it's there again, and when it hits the back of her throat she starts coughing. The nearby diners are watching her now, so she turns away, hiding her face behind her napkin as she hacks so hard that it makes her retch. Looking down at the table there's a small heap of red dust piled on the wood, a fine, ruddy grit that reminds her of the desert. She isn't sure if it's come from out of her, or from somewhere else. When she wipes it away some of it sticks in the creases of her palm, a road map to unknown lands.

*

It's late before she decides to head back to the hotel. She has left her watch in the hotel room, so she isn't sure of the exact time, but it must be getting close to 2 a.m. Most of the bars are closed, but not all of them. She enjoys the dark. When she thinks of returning to her room she imagines uniformed officers waiting in the foyer, removing her belongings in meticulously tagged and documented see-through bags. Her laptop. Her phone.

The image sets her wandering, circling the CBD as if she's in a maze, unable to find her route home. The streets are quiet now. Apart from an occasional burst of drunken shouting as the late bars turn out, she is left to herself. She thinks she sees the homeless man from the other night, slumped beside a bin, but it isn't him. Perhaps he found himself a shelter after all. Perhaps something worse happened.

The sun is just beginning to stain the horizon when she finally gives in. Her feet are sore, the buzz of the alcohol is wearing off. All she wants is to curl up and sleep. The hotel is six or seven blocks away, and she's haunted by the mental image of the police waiting for her, all those bad decisions coming home to roost. In the end, she sits in an empty doorway, hugs her arms about her. The cold is soothing rather than disruptive. Her sleep comes quick, and deep, and long.

*

When she wakes, she knows that something is different. Her clothes feel bulkier. She can't quite make sense of it, but the textures are all wrong. There's that smell too; she assumes she picked a bad doorway to pass out in, one already marked with urine, or vomit, or worse. When she moves her arms are unreasonably heavy, her skin prickling and dry. Her head is unbalanced.

When she looks at her hands, they are not her hands.

The sight makes her sit up. The daylight is brilliant now, piercing everything. There is no room for confusion. She looks down at a man's hands, dark, the fingers thick, the nails squared off and packed with dirt. She turns them over, turns them back. Moves her fingers and watches this man's hand respond. The dizziness she feels is not unfamiliar, but everything else is wrong. As she stands she almost hits her head on the shop sign.

She stumbles half a block before she finds a window that she can see her reflection in. Her feet feel huge, ungainly. She trips and almost sprawls more times than she can count. A man in a blue suit stares at her in disgust, until she realises that she must appear drunk. Beyond that, she has no idea what he sees. It's curiously liberating to have no sense of self-image. She flips him the finger.

The window belongs to a mobile phone shop, the latest models and cases arrayed in ranks against a black background. It's this that casts her reflection, allows her to see her face. She moves one stubby-fingered hand up to brush her cheek, the tips resting on cracked lips. The face that stares back is that of the homeless man, the Aborigine. With her – his – index finger she traces the deep furrow on his – her – forehead. His tongue probes his teeth; the front two are cracked, at least three are missing. His breath whistles out of his nose, like a kettle, or a miniature train. His crotch... well, there's that. It itches. He rearranges his clothes, the stained cargo pants, the parka jacket worn over a stiff, crusted T-shirt. Then he walks.

The hotel is not hard to find. He remembers what it was like to be Miriam, how she moved. He knows all about the stolen money, the failing marriage, the flight that was only ever heading in one direction. The cough that keeps forcing itself up through his throat is all his own, but the way he dabs at his mouth afterwards is hers. He is neither one thing nor another. He doesn't know what he is.

At the taxi rank one of the bellboys bars his way, gently cajoles him back towards the street. He doesn't make a scene of it, and he's grateful of that. Of course, he can't walk here any longer. That privilege is gone. Instead he settles in a vacant doorway opposite, watches the revolving doors. He doesn't know what he expects, but he has nowhere else to go. In a pocket he finds the cheap, plastic sunglasses and he wears them for a while. They pinch his head, though, and eventually he tosses them into a corner. He drifts in and out of sleep, waiting.

They come as the light is waning, the shadows stretching like long-fingered ghosts towards the dusk. Two marked police cars, an unmarked car with officers in suits. He thinks they have come for him, but they don't even glance in his direction. Instead they enter the hotel. Twenty minutes later they're back, the uniforms carrying bags of evidence in their arms. The two suited officers lead a woman to the back of their car. It's Miriam, her hands cuffed behind her, her eyes red, streaked with tear-tracks. Without thinking he reaches out a hand as if he can touch her, as if he can pick her up and put her in his pocket. There is no way to take back what has already gone, though. One officer puts his hand on her head as they guide her into the back of the car. Then the lights flash and the sirens fade.

He stays standing in the doorway for some time, as the light fails around him, as the night creeps in. He has no idea what his name is, no idea of where he comes from. All he knows is that he doesn't belong here. Somewhere out there, beyond the city limits, waits the desert, an antipodean crucible of heat and dust, a place where anyone might be erased. He hikes his trousers up by the waistband and starts walking.

BADDAVINE

I didn't hear the whispers. Not at first. It was Emily who mentioned them, her eyes wide, that impish grin on her face. We'd left Sarah and William back at Summer's Gate, the little man poking a puffball with a stick, watching it expel tiny clouds of spores into the air. Emily and I had carried onwards, through the boggy patch at the start of the bridle path and then a sharp left, pushing aside a low-hanging elder as our mud-caked boots trod an animal track through the winter undergrowth. I'd paused to watch a robin trying to tug a worm free of the claggy soil when she spoke.

'Can you hear him, Daddy?'

I thought she meant the robin at first, and shook my head. 'I think his mouth's full.'

Emily smiled indulgently, as she sometimes did now that she was in year three. As if she had learned everything there was to know about the world, and I was still catching up.

'Not him, silly. The whispering man. I couldn't hear him back at the path, but he's clear now, isn't he?'

Her certainty made me pause to listen. We'd all heard rumours of what went on in the woods at night – the drug use, the bikers – and it didn't sound unfeasible that someone should be hidden nearby in the undergrowth. Maybe more than one someone. But there was nothing, just the soft rustle of dry leaves in the breeze, a sudden, sharp caw in the distance that was most likely a jay or a magpie. The rush of my own blood in my ears, only slightly quieter than them both.

'There's no one there, Em. I can't hear anything.'

She placed a gloved hand over one ear and closed her eyes. I'd assumed it was an act, but was struck by the way she screwed up her face in concentration, her nose wrinkling towards her brow. I was used to most of her tells from the games of make believe she played with her brother, but none of them were showing. It occurred to me that she wasn't making this up, not intentionally.

'He's very quiet,' she said finally, 'but he's definitely there. I can't hear what he's saying though. His voice is too growly. Like a bear, or the Gruffalo in the cartoon.' She smiled at that last part. It was William's favourite, we must have watched it at least ten times over the previous month. It occurred to me that it might be where this fantasy had sprung from.

'Sorry.' I shrugged. 'Maybe he can only be heard by little girls and boys. My old ears are too tired.'

Emily smiled, thrusting her hands back into the pockets of her coat, and we continued on our way. Behind us I could hear William shrieking and thwacking the dead nettles with a stick, Sarah trying to coax him in our general direction. The moment had passed, and I almost forgot about it as we zigzagged our way back home across the common. It was only as we turned onto Pepys Way that I saw Emily pause for a couple of seconds, her head tilted as if listening for something. Then she smiled and skipped after me, content that she'd found what she was searching for.

*

The mob swells as we reach the edge of the common, ten or twelve bodies joining us as we skirt the estate. Word spreads quickly now. I imagine they knew what was happening before we even left The Tankard, the ripples spreading, pulling us all to the same shore.

Torches and mobile phones bob and flicker as we head into the trees, and I find myself falling back, almost ready to disintegrate into the darkness if the mass of bodies were not pulling me along. There's a shout from somewhere up in front, 'Over here!' and the mob flows right, branches and bracken crackling underfoot. I can smell someone's body odour, like rotting onions. A whoop, then we start to run, the lights dipping and darting, descending into chaos. I ignore my aching legs as we hurtle through the night.

Someone shouts, 'We've got him,' squeaking into a falsetto that makes me think he's a teenager, but I have no need of the warning. I can hear it now, we all can. That rumbling whisper growing louder in our heads, gravelly and old. The voice Emily had heard that day in the woods. The creature we had come to call Baddavine.

*

Sarah doesn't like me taking the kids out in the rain, but around eleven it dries to a mist-like drizzle so we tug on our wellies, zip our waterproofs up to our chins, and head up the hill to Wells Gate. Emily is eager to get to the woods but William dawdles as usual, kicking at puddles, stooping to pick up a stick that appears to the naked eye to be no different to any other stick in the world. I can feel the mist painting my face with a cold, damp sheen, but I like it. Emily wipes her forehead with her sleeve and grins.

The gate's entrance has flooded, a deep puddle five feet across and surrounded by thick, sucking mud, so we track in single file past the bramble bushes, their roots having held the clay together. William already has mud smeared up to the top of his wellies, but I pick him up regardless. His soles wipe tracks down the front of my jacket like I've been run over.

I'm about to suggest that we take the paved route today but Emily is already pushing between the trees, following a wide track between stands of collapsed bracken. The path's not as bad as I'd feared, the earth here is less muddy, and I stop for a moment to let William down. As soon as his feet hit the ground he's running ahead and giggling, the stick still clutched in one hand, rattling off tree trunks. He manages to find a small puddle to one side of the path and jumps in with both feet.

Emily has stopped ahead of us. I wonder if she's found something, but as we walk closer, the little man scraping trails through the mud, I see that she has closed her eyes. The realisation blooms that she has brought us back here, where she heard the whispers last week. Her head is tilted, listening. Then her eyes snap open.

'Can you hear him now? Tell me you can hear him, Daddy, or I'll think I'm going mad.'

I want to say no. It would be easier, safer, to dismiss it as the fantasy of a little girl, wrapped up in her imaginary world of unicorns and Pokémon. But when I stop walking and listen, truly listen, tuning my ears to pick up any stray sounds out here in the woods, I do hear something. It's only faint, a low bass rumble tickling my eardrums, rising and falling in intonation like the mounds and ditches of the landscape. Like someone speaking.

I don't know why, but my first instinct is to grab Emily, pull her close. She yelps as my hand closes around her arm, too tight, and I realise what

I'm doing. There is no immediate threat here, nothing to protect the children from. Just a voice whispering on the wind. Still, I hunker down and gather her and William to me, wrapping my arms around their shoulders as all three of us squat in the mud and listen.

'He's saying something, isn't he Daddy? The whispering man? It sounds like words but I can't understand them. Do you think it's Spanish?'

We'd been on holiday to the Costa Brava the previous summer, so it was natural that Emily should assume anything unintelligible was Spanish, but the voice was speaking no language I knew. It was more guttural somehow, like the gurgling of a brook, but harsh, staticky and wild. Screwing my eyes shut, I tried to concentrate on the sounds, the half-words that were forming. I could make out something that sounded like *Badda*, repeated over and over again – *Badda-bada-baaddaaa-ba-bada...* Then a drawn-out wail that made me jump, upsetting my balance and sending me sprawling arse-first in the mud. *Viiiinnne...*

'I think we should go home now,' I said, picking myself up without bothering to brush my trousers down. 'Time to go home.'

*

When I was twelve, I lost all hearing in one ear for a period of almost two months. It came without warning one day on the bus to school – a sudden *pop* in my left ear, then nothing. I could still hear with my right ear, but the bus sounded different somehow, the tyres hissing more insistently against the tarmac of the road, the other children's voices higher-pitched, more manic. I suffered half-heard lessons all day, and when I got home that night Mum told me I needed my ears syringed, implying that I was somehow to blame for the inconvenience, for allowing my bodily fluids to build up so recklessly.

I didn't need my ears syringed. When I saw the doctor two days later he sent me for tests, having found nothing in my ear canal to explain the silence that had descended upon half of my world. A specialist in London proclaimed it a case of SSHL – sudden sensorineural hearing loss – a definition that did little more than describe my symptoms. When it came to causes, they were as baffled as I was. I was given a course of pills to take – steroids, Mum would later tell me – and they had started to talk about hearing aids when the sound suddenly came back one afternoon, in a rush, as we stood in the queue at Sainsbury's. One moment I was stood daydreaming next to our trolley, half-hearing the bustle of the shop about me; the next, there was a dramatic whoosh of noise in my left ear again and everything was as clear as before, perhaps even clearer, loud and bright and utterly overwhelming.

I'm told I collapsed to the floor right there on Aisle 12, and they took me through to the manager's office for a glass of water and a biscuit until the paramedics arrived. They weren't needed, though. I was simply in temporary shock at the chaotic din of everyday life, something everyone else took for granted. I felt slightly dizzy and nauseous for a few days after, but then everything was as it had been before.

Since then I'd been more aware of what a gift hearing is, however, and the suddenness with which it might be taken away. So when Baddavine began whispering to us, it felt like the miracle I'd been waiting for.

*

Some of the mob begin to shout now, their voices rising into the night with whoops and wails, inhuman and raw. I don't understand what they're doing at first, what has transformed this crowd into a pack of animals baying at the moon – but then I realise. They're screaming to try and smother the voice, *his* voice, as it invades their heads. They're creating a wave of sound to drown out Baddavine, to silence him at last.

It doesn't work. The rumbling words remain unchanged, deep and earthy − ...*adda-ba-bada-viiine-bada-vine...* − as if they exist on an entirely different wavelength, the screaming and the shouts slipping off the surface of them like rain. For a brief moment they scream all the louder, desperation raw in their throats, then as one they fall silent. Frustration rises from the mob like a stink and I can feel a charge in the air, the buzz of pheromones being released. The air almost crackles with it.

Baddavine sounds exultant now, rumbling through our heads unimpeded, an impossible voice from the distant past. *Bad-badda-badadda-viiine...*

But whatever he may be, his time has come. I can see that now, we all can. I see it in the raised fists, the cricket bats and garden forks, the carving knives and crowbars. There's no stopping what happens next.

∗

The Tankard wasn't always The Tankard. Back when we were kids it was an old-fashioned sweetshop, Pritchard's, with jars of aniseed balls and lemon bonbons in the window. Then it was a grocery store for a while, with a small magazines section that for some reason stocked an eclectic mix of imported American comics, mainly *Thor* and *Iron Man* but occasionally issues of *Swamp Thing* too. When I was fifteen it closed suddenly, the front boarded up and left to gather graffiti and mould in equal measure. It stayed that way for almost twenty years, until a carpet retailer bought it and refurbished it as a showroom. When that went under two years later, Gareth moved in and The Tankard came into being.

To say that we didn't have a local before that isn't strictly true. There was the Brewer's Arms in Tadworth, the Stirrup and Mane over near the racecourse. But The Tankard filled a space in our community that neither of those had, serving as a home-away-from-home despite the cheap chipboard tables, the poorly filled rough patches on the walls where display racks had once been bolted, the fact that it still felt more like a shop than a pub. That made it ours, and we embraced it from the day it opened.

Plus the beer was good. That always helps.

I wasn't in the habit of making solo trips to The Tankard, but something had been bothering me all day. Once Sarah got home from work, and the kids were tucked away in bed, I buttoned up my coat and braved the elements to walk up the hill.

Gareth was on his usual perch at the end of the bar, his fingers stroking his reddish tangle of beard while Big Mike and Burnsy explained the finer points of England's batting collapse. There were a few other faces I recognised – Mrs Madeleine and her son, Simon; Derek who ran the Under-5s football club that William was signed up for this coming spring – but I made a beeline for the group at the bar. Gareth had in many ways become the barometer of the community, a filter for local news as it flowed in and out of his door. If anyone had heard anything, he'd know.

Burnsy stopped talking and looked my way as I approached, but Big Mike kept on expounding on his theories, placing the blame on everything from England's selection committee to the attitude of the travelling fans Down Under. It was only when Gareth coughed and nodded to me that he paused and turned.

'You look troubled.' That was Gareth, his voice level and relaxed, same as ever. 'Anything we should know about?'

Now that I was here, I didn't know where to start. I'd spent the previous evening sitting in semi-darkness, lit only by the anglepoise lamp on my desk, listening, waiting. When Baddavine's voice had finally come to me I wasn't sure if I was making a breakthrough or going slowly mad.

'This is going to sound crazy…' I could hear the uncertainty in my own voice, the self-doubt, '…but have you guys heard anything lately? A voice, I mean. Out on the common. I don't know how to describe it… a whisper? In your head? Is it just me?'

There was a silence, and I became aware that everyone else in the room had stopped speaking too, their conversations simmering to a stop as they tuned in to what was happening at the bar. This is the point where I finally get sectioned, I thought. This is the point where they call the men in white coats.

I'd been looking to Gareth for an answer, but it was Big Mike who spoke first. His voice always struck me as surprisingly squeaky for such a big man, as if puberty had stalled halfway and his voice had cracked but not broken.

'I've heard it,' he said, and I could sense the whole room listening. 'Not all the time, but sometimes. A deep, raspy whisper, in my head. I can't make out words, mind you, just the voice. That what you mean?'

My relief must have been visible, because Gareth stood up from his stool and placed a hand on my shoulder across the bar. 'You're not the only one, mate. A few of us have.' He lifted his eyes, addressing the room. 'Who here has heard it? The voice he's talking about?'

Murmurs came from all corners, confirming that they'd heard it too.

'I'm not sure what it's saying,' I said, when no one else spoke up, 'but it sounds to me like 'Baddavine'. That's what we've been calling it, me and the kids. Baddavine. I think it's out there, somewhere, hiding in the undergrowth. I think it's calling to us.'

I heard someone repeat the name, 'Baddavine,' and then it became a chorus, echoing about the bar as people tried it out, tasted it for the first time. I might have been imagining it, but somewhere in the back of my head I thought I heard a whispered ...*bada-baddaviiine...* as if the creature had heard us and was responding to our call.

'Baddavine it is, then,' Gareth said, sitting back down and running his fingers over his beard again. 'You've named it. The question now is, what do we do about it?'

*

We find it, eventually, crouched under a tangled thicket of brambles at the back end of the common, near the old cottages on Sundown Lane. It's cornered, trapped between the stream at its back and the mob surrounding it on the three other sides. I don't know about the others, but I can hear its voice clearer than ever now, a grating bass rumble that vibrates inside my head. It sounds different, though. Less stable, more tense. Scared.

...*viiiiiine-bad-bada-ba-baddaviiine...*

The mob is starting to coalesce, the chaos refining, focusing, forming a spearhead. The torches and phone lights that have bounced around the woods in the darkness find their target at last, shining in from all angles upon the thicket. There's a smell of violence in the air, like ozone. I can see something beneath the brambles, a dark mass the size of a Labrador or an Alsatian, but with shorter legs, low to the ground. A scent of animal musk and fear.

'It's moving.'

I'm not sure who shouts that, but it may have been Big Mike, or the teenager from earlier. Whoever it is, they're right. I can see it move too, shifting its bulk in its makeshift hideaway, turning away from the light.

There's a flash of something white, and I realise that it has markings on its fur.

Then someone else shouts, 'It's making a run for it,' and they're right, it's scrabbling through the rotten leaves towards the stream, and we're moving too, our horseshoe formation breaking up as we become a mob again, slipping and sliding down the muddy bank in Baddavine's wake.

I see it properly now, lit up by a constellation of tiny spotlights. It looks a little like a badger, but bigger, denser somehow, its body so low to the ground that it almost seems to flow over the earth. There are two streaks down its sides, like comets against the dark fur, and a short tail that drags through the dirt. Its head is wide, almost as wide as its body, and wedge-shaped, its eyes glinting like dark marbles in the light cast over it.

It's the claws that cause me to stumble and almost lose my footing, though. They are not like any animal claws I have seen, as they scrabble for purchase down the bank. Splayed out from beneath it at front and back, emerging from beneath the straggly fur, they look like human hands, fleshy and jointed, the nails blackened with dirt but nails just like mine nonetheless.

Whatever this revelation means, though, there is no time to act on it. No time to think, or to stop what has already started. The creature – Baddavine – is slow down the slope, and with every scratching scramble of its childlike fingers it loses purchase, the clay beneath it thick and wet. By the time it splashes into the shallow stream, the water barely reaching halfway up its fur, the mob is only a few feet behind, their arms swinging upwards.

Its whisper has become a shout, so loud that I fear my ears are bleeding. As happened in my childhood, when my hearing returned, I start to feel dizzy and slightly sick, the noise rushing over me in a solid wave.

...BAAADA-BAADA-VIIIIII...

They are hitting it now, all of them, with their makeshift weapons, their bats and pipes. There's a wet thud, then another, as their arms swing down, a sound like a spade splitting the earth. The people are silent as they go about their dirty work.

It's a golf club that finishes it in the end. I see Burnsy raising it above his head, and when it comes down there's a sudden *crack* and the voice stops. Just like that, the noise in our heads is silent. I'm so unsteady on my feet that I collapse onto the bank, my arse in the dirt, and watch as everyone catches their breath. Eventually, after a few minutes have passed, four men lift the battered, bloodied slab of meat out of the stream, and between them they carry it back to the town.

*

It's Mrs Madeleine, I think, who suggests that we skin it. Thorngood, the butcher, has kept it in his walk-in fridge for almost a week at this point, while we all caught our breath and wondered what we should do. What we had done. It's in The Tankard one night that she just comes out and says it, and the way she explains it, it makes perfect sense. Her Simon has been taking taxidermy classes for a while now, and he knows how to cure the skin. It's a unique trophy for our local's walls, a curio to remind us of what we witnessed, what we found that night on the common. It might even bring in more trade, Gareth suggests, if word gets out. People might want to see what remains of our creature.

No one calls it Baddavine any more, I notice. We took that name away from it. It's the creature now.

*

The skin hangs on the back wall of The Tankard for close to a year before I take it. At first there are a few curious visitors, encouraged by photos of it on Instagram and Twitter, a tiny two-inch column in the local rag. They take some photos, buy a drink, then leave. A few of them don't even bother with the drinks, and Gareth soon abandons any hope of making his fortune out of it. It simply hangs there, part of the furniture. Big Mike mentions that it has started to smell, and we blame Mrs Madeleine's son for the poor workmanship. The beads he has set into the skull look nothing like those bright, intelligent eyes.

The night I take it, Gareth is preoccupied with changing the pumps, and I'll confess that I've had a few more than was wise. I've been drinking more lately, both in The Tankard and at home. I'm unsteady on my feet as I snatch it from the wall and march towards the door before anyone can stop me, or even notice. They all seem to be staring into their pints, their thoughts elsewhere. I'm not sure why I do it, but it seems to make sense, and as I walk home I run my fingers through the matted fur, trying to remember what it – *he* – was like. I can't help wondering what he was trying to tell us.

It's as I sit in the garage, my legs splayed out across the concrete floor, Baddavine's skull atop my head and his fur resting heavy on my neck and shoulders, that I think I hear it. It's far off in the distance, and the alcohol has created a rushing and fizzing in my ears, but I would swear there is a voice out there somewhere, drawing closer, looking for what it has lost. Something big, and old, moving slowly but inexorably towards our town.

FAR FROM HOME

At Swindon the train filled up, and to his dismay Gary found that his view was now obscured by a lady with an obscenely large pink suitcase. He had spent most of the journey staring at the pristine white linen suit of a gentleman several seats further down the carriage. Now that diversion was denied, he found himself at a loose end. Eventually he discovered a chocolate wafer that had survived a previous family outing, having fallen into an internal pocket of his rucksack, and he gnawed on it as they passed through Bristol Parkway.

A little before four o'clock Lisa called, and he switched his phone to silent. She didn't leave a message. Things weren't exactly difficult between them, but he would admit to being glad of a couple of days away. He always missed the kids, and his wife too, but he'd come to believe that their time apart was just as important as their time together. An extra hour in bed and a full English breakfast – savoured, without interruption – could work marvels.

On disembarking at Cardiff Central, Gary was pleased to spot the familiar white linen jacket weaving through the ticket barriers. It made his journey feel more complete, knowing that his immaculate companion had arrived safely too.

The weather was pleasantly balmy, so he decided to walk. A quick check of his phone suggested a simple route, and he found he was able to follow the flow of people past a series of bus stops to the high street. Painted on the end wall of one of the buildings was a grey mural of a spindly, tube-like creature, its head raised in a cry, or a warning. He couldn't say exactly why but it disturbed him, this unexpected vision. It had to be at least ten stories high. He suspected that it was originally intended as a modern depiction of the Welsh dragon, but the painting had somehow taken on a life of its own. It looked as if it was in pain. As he turned down the high street he could still feel the creature roaring silently at his back.

The hotel was hard to find. It was lucky that he'd written the details on his wrist. The door was hidden in the middle of a parade of shops and pubs, the latter already spilling their clientele onto the pavements as Friday night crawled in. They would be busy once the sun went down. He had to ring an intercom to be buzzed in, a security measure that was both reassuring and slightly foreboding. In the depths of the building he heard a muffled chime.

When the door finally clicked open he pushed through. Inside, Gary found himself standing in a tiled corridor. The light was dim, the only decoration a pair of abstract paintings on opposite walls, thick smears of congealed red across black canvas. It was as he neared the middle of the corridor that he spotted the alcove set into one wall, the lift doors gleaming as if they'd just been polished. There was a laminated sign tacked next to the button, 'Hotel Lobby – 1st Floor'. When the doors closed behind him he found that the control panel only had two buttons, a 'G' and a '1'. There was no option but to press the '1'.

On the first floor a blond woman was seated behind a desk. She smiled as she stood to greet him, and Gary noted with a sense of thrilled intimidation that she was at least a couple of inches taller than him, his eye level resting near her lips. He wondered if the desk might be sitting on a raised platform, or whether she was wearing heels. If not, she must be at least six foot two.

'Checking in are we, sir?'

Her accent was thick, and he had to unpick it to get at the sense of what she'd said.

'Yes, just one night. I have a meeting tomorrow, the Owain Gallery should have booked me a room. I have the number here somewhere.'

He was embarrassed at having written the hotel details on his wrist, and was trying to devise a way of reading them without being obvious when she spoke.

'I have it, I have it here. An artist then, are you?'

She looked him up and down, clearly finding it hard to believe that someone this unfashionable might be involved in the arts.

'No, no. I'm a contractor, we're helping the gallery put together their new space. Multi-purpose hanging fittings, that sort of thing. Nothing exciting. No painting with my piss or anything.'

He wasn't sure why he'd said that last part. It had sounded funnier in his head. The lady sniffed, turning back to her screen. Beneath the desk something whirred.

'I have you in room 114. Down the corridor, no need to take the lift. Turn left at the end, then right at the next corridor, and you'll find it down the bottom. Last room. Your key card opens the front door too, and breakfast is served from seven until nine tomorrow, should you want it. Prices are in your room. Call if you need anything.'

As was often the case when he was away from home, he found himself wondering what she might be like in bed. He'd never had sex with anyone taller than him – in fact, for close to fifteen years he hadn't been naked with anyone other than Lisa – and he found her height both intimidating and erotic. There would be an element of role reversal, he imagined, with her calling the shots. It was only natural given her physical dominance. Unable to decide whether that was something that aroused him or not, he took the key card she had placed on the desk. He did his best not to look at her as he shouldered his bag.

The corridors were longer than he'd expected but the room numbers were clearly signposted at each junction. 114 was the final room in a corridor that led nowhere, tucked back into the dead-end as if someone had bricked it up and only just found space to squeeze in one more bedroom. He had to lean his shoulder against the wall to slide the key card into the slot. At least there would be no drunks staggering past at two in the morning.

As was often the case with hotel rooms, it struck him with both its blandness and its curious idiosyncrasies. The bedside cabinet (small, laminate) was topped with a two-foot-high ornate lamp that looked like an alien lemon juicer, and a tiny, cheap digital clock that couldn't have cost more than a fiver. There was a door on the far side of the bed, but when he tried the handle it was locked. There was no evidence of a keyhole, he noticed, or any clue as to where it might lead. From the layout he imagined that it must connect to one of the other rooms.

The complimentary toiletries were better than average and the bathroom was spotless, so he ran himself a bath. As the water hissed into the tub he stopped at the window. He was surprised to find the grey mural in front of him again, its cold, tubular body contorting across the wall opposite. He had no idea how he had doubled back on himself, but somehow he must have. The hotel corridors had their own strange geography. From this angle, he could see that it was definitely meant to be a dragon of sorts, the Welsh emblem redrawn in twisted metal. That didn't alleviate the impression of a creature in pain, though. He pulled the curtains tight, blocking it out.

The bath was disappointing, too hot and too narrow for him to get comfortable, and after steaming for a few minutes he dragged himself out again. His legs and torso had boiled a bright pink, so he wrapped a towel around his middle while he cooled down and headed back into the bedroom.

At first he thought they were doing renovations or repair work in the adjacent room. The banging was rhythmic, like a hammer, but softer too. The image that came to him was of someone banging their head against the wall over, and over, and over again. At times the pace would quicken and he feared they would come through the plaster. Then the noise would slow and become muffled, until he was uncertain that he'd heard it at all. It was only when someone climaxed with a lingering scream that he finally realised what he'd been listening to. A flush spread across his chest. He half expected to look down and find himself erect beneath the towel. In that department, though, nothing appeared to have stirred.

After a minute or two he crept across to his clothes – not wanting to interrupt the calm that had fallen next door – and pulled them on in silence.

When he left the room he stole a furtive glance at the next door along the corridor, but there was no indication of what might be happening behind it. They hadn't even hung the Do Not Disturb sign on the handle. It was almost as if they wanted someone to stumble upon them in the act.

*

At some point night had fallen, and street lamps now coated the city in a sickly orange glow. When he stepped outside there were more people than before, young men loitering in territorial groups outside the pubs, couples hurrying from place to place on private missions of their own. There was even a hen party jeering and whooping from one of the open-fronted bars, uniformly dressed in pink tutus and cheap plastic police helmets. He might have imagined it, but he thought he saw one of them mimicking fellatio with a plastic truncheon.

He didn't know where to go. There had been a trip to Cardiff once before, in his teens, but he couldn't remember it in any detail. He wasn't even sure what it had been for. The flow of people seemed to swell left more than right, so he allowed himself to be carried along, just another body in the river. It was down a side street that he spied the neon sign for Bar D'Abel. All he really wanted was a beer or two and something to eat. He had to be clear-headed in the morning for the meeting.

The interior of the bar was a pleasant surprise. It was already busy, but compared with the bustle of the high street the room was an oasis of calm. The rear wall glowed with bottles of spirits while two bearded men ruled the bar area, stalking behind it as they tugged on handles and pulled glasses, still steaming, from the drying racks. In the front, three waitresses drifted from table to table, taking orders and clearing empties. The one nearest him was boyish but pretty. There were a couple of tables free, so he seated himself in the corner, out of the way.

It was as the boyish waitress brought him his first beer – a dark ale, close to a porter but dangerously strong – that he spotted the man. In the dim light he stared at him to try and be certain. Yes, it was definitely the man that he'd seen on the train. He remembered the handsome, chiselled look of his features. If that wasn't enough, there was the white linen jacket, draped over the back of an empty chair. The coincidence was remarkable. He considered walking over and introducing himself, but he didn't want to intrude. Instead he hid behind his pint glass.

It didn't take long to realise that something had changed. It was partly in the way the man held himself. His fluid confidence of earlier was now clumsy, as if he was not quite in control of his actions. His shirtsleeves were unevenly rolled up on his forearms, and Gary was disappointed to note that the linen jacket was soiled by two large, black marks on the elbows, as if he'd been crawling on all fours through a peat bog. When one of the waitresses materialised from the darkness the man startled, his panicked look becoming a muttered instruction. She returned a minute later with a pint of thick, dark beer and something smaller and lighter in a straight-sided shot glass. Well, that explained it. The man was clearly a drunk. Gary watched him with a mix of disgust and unexpected longing. There was something to be said for losing oneself in the bottle.

When his waitress returned, Gary ordered a plate of nachos and a second beer. His phone buzzed in his pocket, but he let it vibrate until it simmered back into silence. It would only be Lisa. He surprised himself with his desire not to let her in. The nachos weren't bad and the beer was excellent, but Gary found that his attention kept drifting back to the man's table. He would occasionally mumble something, and Gary wondered whether he was on a hands-free call or was simply rambling incoherently. He couldn't see a phone or an earpiece. At one point he looked as if he was about to stand, then he sat back down abruptly, knocking his jacket to the floor and rattling the empties on the table. He didn't notice the jacket on the floor until the waitress stopped to pick it up. On a call or not, there was no doubt that he was inebriated.

It was only when Gary started his third beer – an IPA, lighter in colour but stronger than either of the others – that he realised just how drunk he was getting. He was used to drinking watery bitters down the local, not these artisan creations. The latest tasted like fortified cough syrup. He hadn't yet lost control, but he felt that he was reaching a tipping point. Another one or two and the night would start to slide away. He could already sense the light from the wall sconces blurring around the edges. There was tomorrow's meeting to consider, and one glance at the state of his travelling companion sealed it. Tonight was a night to stay on the right side of the line.

Having settled with the waitress, he abandoned the last quarter of his pint on the table, stacking three pound coins next to it as a tip. Lisa always called him a cheapskate when it came to tipping, but being in an alien city made him free with his money. He felt that different rules applied. On his way out he passed the man's table, and he risked a glance. There was still no sign of an earpiece, and this close he could see several stains down the front of his shirt, as if some of the drinks had never even reached his mouth. It was depressing to see the transformation, and he wanted to reach out and hug him. Whatever was troubling him, it had clearly pushed him over the edge.

The night was warm, and Gary felt a thin sheen of sweat settle over him as he stepped outside. The streets were more feral than before, the crowds growing increasingly unstable, and he kept his head down as he scuttled back to the hotel. At the front door he had to wait for someone to answer the buzzer, and he could feel the chaotic energy of a Friday night swirling past him, the shouts and the laughter, the sickly-sweet smell of alcohol on the air. Then someone shrieked – a high-pitched, animal yelp – and he turned momentarily to face the street.

The man was there. The man from the train. He stood barely ten feet away, his hands thrust into the pockets of his soiled trousers, his head tipped to the pavement. Gary noticed a pinkish streak of what might be vomit down the front of his jacket. Even though his face was lowered, Gary had the impression that he was watching him, waiting for something. Did he want money? But no, he had seemed well-off when he saw him earlier. There was the jacket, after all. That couldn't have been cheap. Without quite knowing why, a sense of panic settled in Gary's gut like a rock.

They couldn't have been standing like that for more than a few seconds, but when the intercom buzzed and the door clicked open Gary pushed through into the hotel with a sense of urgency. He stood in the tiled corridor and watched the door shut behind him, the man remaining on the other side. His breathing slowed gradually as he waited for the lift, letting it carry him up to the hotel above. By the time the doors opened into the foyer, he felt that he might have overreacted. Probably the beer at work.

The front desk was empty now, and as he shuffled past, Gary wondered who had buzzed him up. He had half hoped that the tall woman would be there again. While he knew that he would never risk approaching her, seeing her might have fuelled the fantasy at least. As he passed the hotel doors on his way to his room, daydreaming that she might be lying in his bed, waiting for him, memories resurfaced of the sounds from next door earlier in the evening. He hoped there would be no repeat of it during the night.

But when he turned into the short corridor leading to Room 114, Gary suddenly stopped. The beer and nachos threatened to force their way back out. Someone was at the door to his room. No, not someone – *him*. There was no mistaking the stained linen suit, even with his back turned. How was it possible that he had reached this floor before him? Was there a back stair somewhere? Gary felt he should say something, point out the gentleman's mistake. They might laugh about it and go their separate ways.

There was the faint *swish* of a key card being swiped through the door lock, the *beep* of acceptance. The man walked through the open door into Gary's room.

There was no doubt that it was his room – there was his bag against the wall, his towel discarded on the bed – but that made even less sense. Everything was starting to spin, as if the entire hotel was tilting into a sinkhole, sucking them down into the earth. There was a strong smell of fresh paint, or maybe tar. The man was taking his jacket off now, shrugging it off in a way that made it look as if he had dislocated his shoulders, the joints bending back further than they should. He turned, and in that instant he was looking directly at Gary, finally, staring at him with an intensity that bordered on hunger. With a single finger, he beckoned to him. Then slowly, casually, he peeled back his sleeve, peeled back his skin, and stretched out a metallic, tube-like limb.

*

The following morning, Gary took his bag with him to breakfast. The meeting wasn't scheduled for another four hours, but he'd find a café somewhere, or a bar. Maybe he'd just walk for a while.

He had woken famished, his stomach a growling pit, so reserving a table with his bag he filled a plate with bacon, eggs, black pudding, the works. It was as he sat down that he finally saw the figure hunched in the corner. The man sat with his back to him, but there was no mistaking the white linen jacket draped over the back of the chair, now curiously clean, almost glowing under the stark hotel lights.

Gary sat slowly, quietly, and ate his full English breakfast. He didn't look up until the plate was clean.

FOREIGN LAND

Juin

When she saw the face at the window, Judith screamed.

Looking back on the incident later that morning, with the benefit of two cups of coffee and a smorgasbord of local pastries – not to mention the jams, which she'd already begun to smuggle back on the Eurostar like vials of some contagious disease – she felt that her reaction was not unwarranted. True, Martin's thoroughly unpleasant visage hadn't helped. His thick, wet tongue had been pushed hard into one corner of his mouth, glistening between his lips. After her outburst he'd stood at the window for a few seconds, staring. Then he had nodded and muttered something under his breath before heading off across the lawn. Judith thought it was 'Bonjour,' but it was hard to be sure.

Dominic, of course, insisted that she was overreacting.

'The man was probably just being friendly,' he explained, spraying flakes of croissant across the tabletop while Tim and Rebecca worked their way through a *tres grande* jar of Nutella. 'It's the French way. He was recommended, remember? Don't let your imagination run away with you.'

They had bought the cottage for £104,000 and change, the cost of one of the bedrooms and half the bathroom of their home in Kent. Judith had done the sums. In Falaise that converted to three bedrooms, two bathrooms (one with shower), kitchen, sitting room, dining room (with view), garage, and a number of outhouses, barns and sheds across 208 acres, mostly dilapidated and uninhabitable. And, almost as if he was part of the *terroir*, a gardener: Martin.

Whatever Martin did with his time, it didn't seem to involve much gardening. Occasionally he'd appear in one of the fields, shambling through the long grass with his rusted machete dangling from one hand, but where he had been or where he was heading to was unclear. It was never officially agreed, but somehow the garage had become his domain.

Judith had been wary of the machete since they'd first seen it – it seemed unnecessarily archaic, a crude reminder of the countryside's brutality – and she was dismayed to notice it in his hand when she finally caught up with him that afternoon. She'd spotted him skulking through the knee-high weeds behind the garage, but she didn't notice the blade until she was too close to turn back.

'Martin! Bonjour!'

Having hailed the man she had no idea what to say next, or how to begin to formulate a sentence. Aware that those wide, red-rimmed eyes were on her, she waved in the general direction of the house.

'This morning? I saw… Did you… I mean, perhaps, did you want something? Vous voudrais…?'

Martin's upper lip twitched with what may have been a smile, or might

as easily have been a nervous tic. Then the hand holding the machete
began to lift, and her mind sprang immediately to the children, as if it took
something this barbaric, a blade, to awaken her maternal instinct. Then
came a sense of her own isolation. She had occasionally wondered whether
the gardener had a wife somewhere, although it was hard to imagine, so
grotesque was his appearance. Surely a wife would have straightened him
out. It seemed more likely that he frequented the young girls they'd seen
lining the back streets of Caen on night trips, their skirts barely a few
inches wide, their mouths scarlet and glistening under the streetlamps.
With that thought came the mental image of the misshapen gardener
unclothed, sweating and groaning on top of a young body. Judith flushed.
It seemed too horrible a thing to even imagine.

Martin lifted the blade close to his face, tapping the point against his
temple. She stood transfixed, watching the red-brown tip push tiny divots
in the oily surface of his skin. It seemed certain that he would slip at any
moment and take out his own eye. But he merely mumbled something
unfamiliar and turned away, leaving her staring at his formless, sweat-
stained back. With his free hand he reached around and hiked up the
waistband of his trousers, then he walked away across the field.

Judith stood in the same spot for a few minutes, catching her breath.
She watched him as he stumbled over the molehills, eventually
disappearing through a gate in the far hedge that she thought might lead
to the hilltop beyond, although she wasn't entirely sure. In all that time he
didn't once look back. But when Judith turned and walked towards the
house she could feel eyes watching her from somewhere, and a shallow
shiver spread across her skin.

*

Octobre

It was to be the last trip of the year, a final lazy weekend before they fastened the shutters and abandoned the French house for the winter. Dominic had floated the idea of spending *Noël* there, but neither of them was sure that a couple of heaters would keep the house warm, and they weren't keen to find out.

As their car crawled up the driveway Judith noticed that the fields had started to invade the property. A vine-like plant had snuck between the flagstones of the patio, creeping its way up the wall. The patio itself was strewn with leaves and what looked like clumps of dried grass. Even the moss on the roof looked thicker than before, despite the oven of the summer. She wondered why they bothered employing Martin, if it looked like this when they arrived. She vowed to bring it up with Dominic later that evening.

In the end, though, the thought went unsaid. Their evening was spent trying to coax a large brown toad out of the kitchen. Tim and Rebecca found it hilarious – Tim especially, running in circles around the kitchen belching his best toad impersonation – but Judith thought the creature was repulsive, with its rubbery, wart-covered back and bulbous eyes. When Dominic finally shooed it out onto the patio with an old coal shovel she found herself quite exhausted by the whole ordeal.

To her surprise she slept late the next morning. She woke in a cold and empty bed, the clatter of plates and squeals of laughter coming from downstairs.

Dominic smiled as she staggered through to the kitchen. He was dressed, cradling a baguette from the village bakery under one arm as he shepherded the children to the table. 'Sleep well, did we? You looked peaceful, so I thought it best to leave you. We've been shopping.' He made the final statement with a flourish, as if he expected her to be impressed. 'No sign of the gardener yet either, which might explain the state this place was in. If we need to hire a new one in the new year, then so be it. Coffee or tea?'

The children had discovered an old cardboard carton of broken sticks of chalk in one of the cupboards, and they were busy most of the morning drawing on the patio flagstones. Rebecca was occupied with a hopscotch grid, shuffling back and forth, back and forth like a wind-up doll. Tim was scribbling some kind of narrative on the stone, like a caveman leaving mysteries for future generations. There was a knight, and their car, and what may have been a dragon or a dinosaur. Someone was undoubtedly in peril. They seemed happy.

After a light lunch of more baguette and a slab of British cheddar, the children went back outside to their games. They had planned to uproot them for the necessary visit to the local *supermarché*, but they looked so peaceful that Dominic offered to do the trip solo. His French was improving faster than Judith's, and he was more than capable of picking up the few essentials to see them through the weekend. His last instruction to Judith was to put her feet up and enjoy the quiet. The children were occupied, the sun was out, and they were meant to be on holiday after all. There was an unspoken assumption that she'd somehow earned it.

So she did just that. After she'd watched the car creep down the driveway she checked on the children one last time, then she poured herself a generous glass of Grenache and collapsed onto the sofa with a book. It was a murder mystery she had started several months earlier but she hadn't picked it up in weeks, and the plot proved too complex on a second visit. After ten minutes she dropped the book on the floor and quickly, deliberately, fell asleep.

At one point she stirred, half waking from a dream about a toad with the face of a cow, and in a daze she thought she saw a figure at the window. Her first thought was that it must be Dominic returned from the shopping trip, but the shape was all wrong, shorter and wider than her husband. It took her a few seconds to recognise Martin. Her only thought was that they'd have to have a conversation with him soon, about not continuing his contract next year. She raised a hand in greeting, and was asleep again almost before it collapsed back to her side.

When she finally woke she knew that something was wrong. The light outside looked different now, a sickly orange glow that turned her skin yellow, and as she staggered through the kitchen she felt as if she might throw up. There was no noise from outside. Pushing out into the waning light she found the patio empty. Rebecca's hopscotch grid was scuffed across the stones. Tim's drawings were still there, but it looked as if he'd abandoned them partway through sketching a castle, the drawbridge half drawn, the moat missing. The chalks lay where they'd dropped them, and as a light breeze stirred they *plinked* hollowly on the uneven surface.

Judith took a breath. She must try to be logical. Dominic had come back early, that was all. She couldn't see the car, but he might have taken them out again, or parked it down by the lane and walked up. It was then that she thought to check her phone, and with relief she saw a text from her husband. That explained everything. She tapped the icon to open it, in case she could meet them. The day wasn't over quite yet.

Delayed in town. Do we need more bread?

She gripped the phone in her fist. 'Tim? Rebecca?' Nothing, not even a rustle among the leaves. It was only then that she remembered her dreamlike vision, half awake, of Martin's leering face. She took off at a run.

The garage door was open, swinging in the breeze. The gardener had definitely been to the house, then. She hadn't imagined it. But when she looked inside the space was empty. His crate stood where it always had, the tools were still arrayed along the wall. She had no idea if they were all there. Her phone had a flashlight app, so she switched it on and shone it around. The rusted mechanisms of an old lawnmower in the corner. An empty sandwich wrapper on the crate. Then it illuminated a large, dark stain on the concrete and she stopped. It looked black, maybe dark red. No way of telling if it was new or not.

Judith backed out onto the grass, her hands shaking. The phone fell to the ground as she started yelling in earnest, screaming the names of her children over and over until her throat was hoarse and she had to stop. The land remained unmoved, drowning her in its inscrutable silence.

When her voice finally gave in she sat in the long grass, alone, and waited for Dominic to return.

ONES AND ZEROS

Standing in the porch she swears she can feel the building leaning, a camber to its moss-shrouded bricks that doesn't quite follow the lie of the land. The bay windows at the front of the cottage lean the other way, doubling the effect. She feels slightly queasy. Her fingers find the key in her handbag and she slides it into the lock. She traces the cast-iron numbers screwed into the oak door – '10' – then she turns it, feels the rusted tumblers fall into place and settle once again.

'Hello? Alan?'

She knows he's here somewhere, his Volvo is sitting on the drive, shaming her scraped, rusted Cortina, but there's no answer. The cottage squats in silence. For a moment she imagines something has happened to him, some horrific accident, but with an effort she pushes the thought away. It's a technique the therapist taught her – the third one, the goatee man – this visualisation of rejecting a fear, taking it in her hands and thrusting it away from her. Sometimes it works; other times, the fear is stronger than the visualisation.

'Alan? Are you there? Hello?'

The floorboards overhead let out a creak and she half expects him to come thumping down the stairs, grinning as always, full of life. Only more silence follows. Then a shout from the kitchen at the far end of the corridor.

'I'm down here, Sis. Come give me a hand, will you? Damned tap's leaking.'

She staggers as she walks down the corridor, seasick on dry land, and she reaches out a hand to steady herself. The wallpaper is cool and slightly damp beneath her fingertips. Without thinking she wipes her fingers on her cardigan.

He's standing at the sink, the tap dismantled on the work surface beside him, doing something with a spanner. A toolbox sits open on the other side of the room, under the boiler.

'Grab me a wrench, will you? That's the one… no, that one… yes. Thanks, Sis. I'll get this fixed for you then leave you to it. The movers have dumped your boxes in the front two rooms, for whatever reason. You'll find them easy enough. You get down here alright?'

When she doesn't answer he looks up at her, his receding hairline glowing in the sunlight from the window.

'You okay?'

'Does the cottage seem straight to you?' She doesn't know why she says it, it just comes out. This happens sometimes, when she isn't paying attention. She tells herself to get a tighter grip. 'I mean, it isn't leaning is it? It felt like it was leaning, when I was outside, and I've read about subsidence online. Clay shrinkage. There's a crack I thought I saw…'

Alan lets the spanner fall with a clatter into the sink and he takes her hand in his, leads her over to a wooden chair. It wobbles as she sits. Now that it's nestled within his, she feels her own hand shaking.

'We got all the surveys done, remember? All and then some. The place is solid, it's stood for close to three hundred years. It's just different is all. You're not in the city now, Sis. Just give it a bit of time. It's bound to feel strange.'

She knows he's right. Of course he is. Good old dependable Alan; not at all like his younger sister.

'You just sit there. I'll fix you a cup of tea, as soon as I can find the box with the kettle in. It'll all be fine, you'll see.'

∗

She doesn't have to start work at once. The mortgage payments are half what she was paying back in the city and her accounts are looking healthier than they have in months. The therapist had suggested it might be good for her, though, and she has clients waiting. Some tweaks to a website, a batch job for a startup in Leeds. It's better than sitting and worrying about the cottage, she knows that. An active mind is a healthy mind.

Once her laptop is unpacked she sets up a workspace on the kitchen table, makes a pot of tea, opens a packet of HobNobs. It's a comfort to settle back into the dev work again, to lose herself in the lines of code, the binary world that she prefers. There's an order to it – when programs go wrong, they obey rules, they follow reason. There's an explanation for everything.

She loses three hours to the website job, the teapot stone cold by the time she finishes. She's almost unaware of where she is until she logs out and turns off. Then she stares around the room, takes in its low ceiling, the stained oak of the window frames. It's almost dark outside, the light thick and brown. Her eyes find a crack in the corner of the room, follow it across the ceiling – no thicker than a thread, but a crack nonetheless.

What was it Alan had said? The surveys were fine, all fine. No reason to worry. Push it away.

It's as she clears the biscuit crumbs from the tabletop that she hears it. A bang, but muffled, like a car door outside, or a cupboard slamming shut elsewhere in the house. She stops, rooted. Silence now. Only her own breath, the thudding of her heart. She waits a minute or more before she calls out.

'Alan? Hello?'

There's no one there. Nobody answers. He wouldn't be here, of course – he has something with the kids tonight, a parents' evening, some such responsibility. Still, she waits another minute. There's a creaking somewhere, like feet moving softly over boards. It stops, then starts again, the cottage shifting in its sleep.

'Hello?'

She stands at the table until the light fails, then she flicks the switch and sets about making her supper.

*

'I heard something, I swear I did. I'm not imagining this. There's either someone here, or something moving in the house, or the house itself... I don't know. But there were sounds, yesterday and today. I don't know what to do.'

She can hear his sigh at the other end of the line. When he speaks it's in his slow, gentle voice, the one he always uses to talk her back from the edge.

'We've been through this, Sis. There's no one there. It's just an old place, remember? Buildings shift a little in their old age, make all sorts of noises. It's just the cottage settling.'

'But you said it was fine. The surveys—'

'The surveys are all good, the noises are perfectly natural. It's just old. Listen, do you need me to come over? Shelley's at work still, but once she gets back she can have the boys. I could be there, maybe eightish?'

She stares at the wall. She knows he's been so kind already, so helpful, but she can hear that patience starting to fray. When she made the decision to move out of the city, to relocate to the country, twenty miles from her brother, it was with the understanding that he could help her if she needed him. If things started to unravel again. But she knows that there will come a point when he stops answering the phone.

'It's okay. I'm okay. You're right, I'm probably imagining things. Blood sugar's probably low. I'll make dinner, put some music on, maybe unpack some more boxes.'

'You know I'm here if you need me? It's just a strange place. Somewhere new. You'll get used to it. The house isn't moving, there isn't anyone there. Until I turned up no one had set foot in it for months. You should have seen the dust bunnies I rounded up. Just give it time.'

She wants to ask him about that, too. Not the dust, but the fact that it was empty. There had been a woman in the cottage before, middle-aged, single. It was the estate agent who gave them all the details, his mouth running and running as if the more words he said, the more tightly it sealed the deal. Her uncle was selling the place because she'd disappeared. Done a runner, they thought; half her clothes gone, the house left abandoned. Something about irregularities at the bank where she worked. The estate agent had made a joke about her sunning herself on the Costa Brava. She wasn't sure how the uncle had been given power of attorney, but he had, and it meant there was no chain, an easy sale. Sitting in her flat in Islington, four thin walls packed tight about her, it had all made sense.

She doesn't ask him, though. She knows he will only sigh again, start wondering if he should be calling the men in white coats. It's unlike him not have asked her about the pills.

'Thanks Alan,' she says, keeping her voice as level as she can. 'I'm just nervous I guess. Give Shelley my love.'

After she hangs up she tips the contents of her pill bottle out onto the kitchen table, a Morse code of little dots and dashes. She singles one out, pushes it around with her finger, then snatches at it and swallows it dry. She sits for a while and listens to the floorboards groaning overhead, and tries not to imagine a woman's feet pacing up and down.

*

That night she hears a baby crying, the noise waking her from a restless sleep. It seems a part of her dream at first, but then she's awake and it's real, the wailing cries rising in pitch as if it's in pain. Her first thought is that it's the woman's baby, but there has never been any mention of a child. And the woman isn't here, she reminds herself. There is nobody here.

The closest house is almost a mile away but the cries continue, until she convinces herself that someone has left a baby outside her door, an infant in a cardboard box, abandoned, scared. She never queries why someone would do this, whose child it is – she simply accepts it as fact. Bustling into her dressing gown she runs downstairs, turns the key in the lock and tugs at the door. It sticks in the frame for a moment and she has to pull even harder, the wood eventually coming unstuck without warning, the door banging against the wall.

There's a flash of russet as a pair of foxes bolt away, their fur a copper blur in the light from the porch. There is no box, no baby. She stands and stares at the dark, half expecting something – someone – to step out of it. Behind her the house moans like a ship settling against the storm.

As she closes the door she runs her fingers over the cool metal of the numbers again, the one and the zero. That is how life should be, in her head: binary; on or off; real or not. Something is or it isn't. There are no shades of grey. Life should be like one of her programs, obeying rules that she can learn, its problems fixed with a new line of code. She knows that isn't the case, but only because she has been told so time and time again by her therapists, her brother. In her heart it still feels true.

It takes her almost three hours to fall back to sleep. When the sun is starting to blush on the horizon she swings her legs over the side of the mattress, twists the cap from the pill bottle. She isn't sure how many she tumbles into her hand, how many little zeros. Ten, perhaps. Maybe more. They're tough to swallow all together, and she crunches them between her teeth, their powder dry and bitter.

At the point where she is tumbling into unconsciousness she thinks she feels the cottage shift beneath her, a beast settling its bulk. In her sleep she grips the sheets to keep from falling out.

*

When she wakes it is almost lunchtime and she's starving. Her stomach grumbles as she pulls her clothes on, and she thinks she hears the cottage murmur a growl in response, sharing her hunger. Staggering down the stairs they feel uneven and she almost trips.

The front door is wide open. She's certain she closed it last night. Didn't she? It can't have swung open by itself, the door is too tight in the frame. There's a scattering of leaves on the hall floor, though, so it must have been open for a while. She pushes it closed, the wood shrieking against the frame as she leans her weight against it. This time she waits to hear the latch click.

'Alan?'

The hole in her stomach has become something else now. She worries she might be sick. It's more than just emptiness; more like a whirlpool inside her, sucking everything down. Her head is fuzzy, and she braces herself against the wall.

The corridor looks wrong, the angles skewed as if it hasn't quite been put together right and the walls don't meet the floor, the ceiling pressing down towards her. There's a creaking like she hasn't heard before, louder and deeper, something rending in the foundations, and then the right-hand wall slides away beneath her hand. One moment it's there, the next it isn't. It's fallen back and to the side, opening a black doorway where once there was brick and mortar, the wallpaper shredded, fluttering in a musty breeze blowing in from who knows where. She blinks and stares, a scream drying up and withering in her throat.

Now she is sick, the paltry contents of her stomach erupting from between her lips, spattering onto the floor. She tries to calm her breathing, pull some air into her dusty lungs. Her skin feels clammy and tight. Somewhere nearby there is the sound of footsteps, quiet but firm on bare floorboards, and without warning five cold fingers interlace with hers. The hand leads her towards the black doorway and, after a moment's pause, she follows without looking back.

*

Alan drops by the cottage after work, Shelley having begrudgingly agreed to pick the boys up from rugby. He hasn't heard from his sister in almost three weeks. It's been worrying him for at least half that time, but he's been reluctant to insert himself into her life, to take on the burden. Shelley has told him enough times that he's too soft on her, that she needs to learn to look after herself. But he knows his sister's not well, and he has to check, so he incurs her scorn and makes the drive out to the cottage all the same.

The grass at the front is almost knee-high, he notes as he pulls into the drive, but that's no surprise. She never was that great at looking after herself. It looks like foxes have been at it on the lawn, the grass flattened in rough circles, what appears to be a lamb bone chewed and discarded to one side. He makes a mental note to have a word with her about weighing down the bin lids.

The door is closed but the latch isn't on, and it opens easily beneath his touch. There are leaves strewn across the hall floor. The air smells stale, blocked up drains and sour milk, and for the first time he's truly worried.

'Sis? You there? Anyone home?'

The house creaks but otherwise there is silence. As he steps back outside and starts thumbing the buttons on his mobile, he notices that the number one is missing from the front door. The zero hangs there alone, an open mouth caught in a silent scream.

NO ONE'S CHILD

The bombs fell on Battersea, crushing it into the dirt, and I was sent away. No one suggested that it was my fault – I knew it was the Germans; I wasn't a stupid girl, not in the slightest – but I couldn't shift the feeling that some undisclosed misdemeanour meant I was no longer welcome. Father bawled his eyes out at Euston, as was often his way, but Mother remained dry-eyed and stern throughout. My last memory of her is of a small, slightly shabby woman standing on the platform with her hands clasped under her armpits. She turned and walked away before my train even left.

The journey felt like an age, but I didn't pay it too much mind. I was a dreamy child even then, prone to drifting off into fantastical worlds peopled by the characters and monsters from my reading obsessions, my mind still too young to truly create anything. If you had seen me, sitting silent in the train carriage with my slender hands clasped in my lap, you would have seen only a pale, undernourished girl, her floral dress at odds with the serious expression on her face. I wore my hair long back then, and straight, so you may not have seen my expression at all. But within I was battling elves, or adventuring with Moonface and Mr Pots and Pans up the Faraway Tree. The fields and the hours just flew by.

I remember that Mrs Hardcliffe didn't meet me at the station, when I finally alighted. She sent a man, to carry my small case and to drive me to the house. I don't recall who, although I suspect it was Hugo. It would have been like her to send her most surly, taciturn servant to collect the little city girl. I didn't care. I was still elsewhere, creating my own friends.

Of those first few months I remember very little. They were not exactly dull – for someone who grew up in a two-up, two-down terrace, Montcastle House offered plenty of amusement – but they inevitably paled into insignificance in the shadow of what happened later. I had been reading C.S. Lewis, I remember, and spent the best part of a week searching for an abandoned wardrobe and the door to another world. There was no other world, though, and it soon became clear that Hardcliffe ruled this one in tyrannical fashion. Hugo's silence was not unusual, and most of the serving staff were so beaten into submission – verbally, if not physically – that they rarely spoke, whether in Hardcliffe's presence or not. I gathered that the young men on the staff had all gone off to the war, and it was the generally held opinion that they had the better deal.

There is one incident that stands out in my memory. In all likelihood its predominance is coloured by the events that followed in its wake, but that is by the by. Nothing in this life remains unstained by our moments of greatest trauma, or so I have come to believe.

Mrs Hardcliffe was not a large woman. Reading back over this, I fear I may have given that impression, but her dominance over that household was of a different kind. She seemed ancient to me, her hands wrinkled and dry like crepe, her body skeletal except where it sagged around the breasts

– but I suspect she was only a little over sixty, if that. To a girl of ten, she looked impossibly old.

I remember she was reading a newspaper while Agatha served breakfast. Which broadsheet I don't recall, although I do remember the two hard-boiled eggs on her plate, impeccably smooth and white on the porcelain. She folded the paper, presumably to read something on the other side, and it revealed to me a large cartoon that dominated the page facing me. I had no concept of satirical art at the time, but I'm sure it had a biting subtext, a pithy caption lampooning our fearless leaders. If it did, it was wasted. All I saw was the image: a gigantic bomb falling through the skies above London, Big Ben visible in the background, and on its rounded tip a leering, malicious face, teeth bared, eyes wide and insane.

The image shocked me. I had seen first hand the damage the bombs were causing, but this – this seemed more real, somehow, than all the fractured buildings, the homes ripped open to the dusty air. To a mind raised on fantasy and imagination, it made more sense, in some perverse fashion. I had no difficulty understanding monsters. I choked on my toast, coughing half of it, pulped and stodgy, back onto my plate.

Hardcliffe lowered the paper, her eyes locked on mine. 'We use a napkin in this household, and we cover our mouths. If you cannot learn this…' She left the thought hanging as she turned the newspaper and saw the cartoon that had shocked me so. My memory may be embellishing, but I'm certain I saw a smile crackle across her thin lips.

'Does this scare you?' she asked, holding the cartoon out towards me, so there could be no doubt what we were discussing. 'It should. War is a brutal thing and those who are weak have much to fear. You are concerned for your mother and father, I would imagine, and rightly so. There is every likelihood that they will die during the bombing, and then you will be an orphan. Your fears are very real. You should be grateful that you are here instead, and thank the Lord that I was generous enough to take you in.'

I had already worked out that when she spoke of the Lord, she actually meant for me to thank her, but I remained silent. She had badly misjudged my feelings and the source of my concern, but I was disinclined to set her right.

Agatha cleared away my dirty plate, replacing it with a new one, and the rest of the meal passed in the usual silence. It was only a week or two later that the telegram arrived with news of my parents' death, but I can't say that it affected either me or Mrs Hardcliffe in any significant manner. Not emotionally, at least. There was a twinge at the thought that I would never again be hugged close to my father's chest, enveloped in his fug of tobacco and cheap soap, but given that I always dreaded those suffocating embraces it struck me as no great loss. My mother barely entered into my thoughts at all.

The one lasting effect of the news was of a practical nature. Shortly after the arrival of the telegram, I was told that Hardcliffe had applied to adopt me as her daughter, and the application had been granted. I can only guess at her motivations for doing so, but given the relentless disdain she showed me I must assume that she drew pleasure from having someone else in the house to reign over, someone without the option of handing in their notice to quit. Perhaps there was some small part of her that regretted never having a child of her own, leaving this world without an heir to maintain her legacy – but if this was the case, she never showed it.

It was soon after that she moved me into the nursery room, with its barred windows and heavy oak door. I didn't mind the nursery itself. The bed was hard, but marginally less so than the one I had endured so far; the shelves were stocked with dusty, leather-bound volumes of poetry and fairy tales that kept me occupied whenever I grew bored. For all that I loved their strange worlds of curses and fey folk, however, the move brought with it a sense of permanence that I could not help but rail against. I could not escape – I had nowhere and no one to escape to – but I would still push against those walls as if she had locked me in a prison. It didn't take long before my urge manifested as a surlier, more combative attitude towards my severe new guardian, and a desire to explore every cobwebbed inch of Montcastle House and make it my own.

So it was that I discovered the cellar rooms.

Hugo had been tasked with keeping an eye on me that day, but as was often the case he had been called away to some urgent matter; a problem with the engine of the motor car, I think. Whatever the reason, I was left alone and I intended to make the most of it. My explorations had already ranged across the first floor – where the nursery room was situated, in the east wing – so as soon as I found myself alone I made my way to the ground level. Most of the rooms here were intended for public viewing, on those rare occasions when Mrs Hardcliffe received guests, rendering them elegant, pristine and irredeemably dull. The dust-free sideboards and serving trolleys shone with disappointment. It was only by chance that I pulled aside a heavy curtain in one of the east wing corridors and found a door behind it. Unlike the other doors this one was scratched in places and the handle looked worn and slightly grubby. My interest, needless to say, was piqued. I discovered it was unlocked, and when I pushed it open it revealed a flight of stone stairs leading below ground. The lack of natural light meant that I could only see five or six steps down, but I knew where Agatha kept the candles and quickly availed myself of one. Clutching it before me, I descended into the darkness.

That there was nothing of any consequence to be uncovered in the cellar rooms did little to dilute my fascination. Their stonework was rough, the candlelight throwing every slight imperfection into stark relief, and this very crudeness was part of their undeniable appeal. It delighted me that the House should rest upon such coarse foundations. But I was equally bewitched by the dark itself, the heavy shadows thrown by sacks of flour on the shelves in one of the rooms, the impenetrable inkwells of the corners where my meagre flame couldn't reach. I had always loved a mystery, and here – away from Hardcliffe's sanitised world, her mannered propriety – the mysteries grew in the darkness like mould. I had no doubt that there were secrets in this basement world, and that I was the one to find them.

Despite the strength of my desire for adventure, however, I almost didn't see him at first. The room at the far end of the subterranean corridor was adorned with all manner of hooks and spikes in the ceiling – presumably for joints of meat to be hung from, dry and bloodless, until they were desired – and these occupied my attention, the flame casting their shadows long and wicked on the stonework. I was so in awe of this overhead armoury that I neglected to look in the corners. It was only when something glinted metallic in the candlelight that I shone my flame, and my attention, in that direction.

I would not, even now, describe him as a man. He had arms and legs the same as you or I, a protuberance on top that might be called a head, but beyond that the similarity ended. To start with, he was barely more than four feet high. If he had been more human, that alone would have bought him service in a travelling freakshow, but his skin – or hide, or shell, or *covering* – had a grey metallic sheen to it that looked like nothing more than a tarnished serving dish. I would have thought it as hard and as rigid as steel, had he not shuffled to hide away from the light, his body flexing and moving like a living thing.

Then there was his head, if such a term can be used. It rose like a moulded dome from his shoulders, curved and smooth, flawless apart from a narrow slit that I took, correctly, to be his mouth. There were no eyes I could see, no ears, no nose. Just that wide slit to mark his face, and as I watched he opened it to let out a rasping yell, the sound pulled from deep in his throat like the shriek of machinery grinding against itself. Inside, I could just make out two dense rows of spiked teeth, pointed and vicious as nails.

I should have run. Back up the stairs, closed the door – never looked back. That would have been the rational thing to do. But I had never been a rational kind of girl. It struck me from the start that he was just as scared as me as I was of him, and that if I was in any immediate danger it more likely stemmed from Hardcliffe discovering my abscondment, rather than this creature squatting in ruined darkness. So, in that moment, I decided that I would make him my friend and ally. I sat down in the dirt, placing the candle in front of me, and waited.

It didn't take long for his fear to mellow. It was clear, I am sure, that I was of no immediate threat. I was nothing more than a young girl, alone in the dark. I don't doubt that something had happened in his past to make him fear humankind, but there was no reason for his fear to extend to me. It took little more than a minute for him to start creeping forward out of the shadows, walking upright like a man but tentatively, ready to drop into a crouch should the situation require it. I would swear that his head tilted ever so slightly to one side, as if he was regarding me with curiosity, although what he used to see me was unclear.

When he finally reached out and touched my hand I was shocked by the coldness of his fingers. They stung as if I had plunged it into a frozen lake, and it was all I could do not to recoil. I sucked in my breath and took his hand in mine, though, his digits short and thick between my slender fingers, and gradually I felt some of my warmth transfer. In this way our partnership was born.

I didn't feel the urge to name him that day, and while it may seem strange to you, I have never once in all this time thought of him as anything other than 'the creature'. You should not take this as a sign of denigration, or servitude. Hardcliffe, after all, knew her servants' names only too well, spitting them from between her dry lips at her every displeasure. It was simply that he didn't require a name, was too divorced from our everyday world to fit within its restrictive nomenclature. To name him would have been to confine him, to constrain him with the power of definition. He was simply the creature, with all the wildness and strangeness that implies.

For the first few weeks I left him where he was, sneaking down the stairs whenever an opportunity presented itself to keep him company, and, to some extent, to remind myself of his existence. If Agatha noticed the gradual attrition of her candle supply, she never mentioned it. Sometime in the second week it occurred to me that he might be hungry, so I snuck into the kitchen when cook's back was turned and grabbed armfuls of whatever I could lay my hands on in the larder: cheese, a heel of bread, apples, a shank of lamb, cooked but still raw and bloody by the bone. He regarded the apples with suspicion, and nibbled at the cheese and bread before pushing them away, but the lamb he ate with undisguised relish, gnawing at the bone with those nail-like teeth of his until there wasn't a shred of flesh left. Taking it back, I could make out a tracery of scratches across the surface, a splinter or two missing in places, presumably swallowed down with the meat. I made note of his carnivorous appetite, stored it away for later. The rest we left to rot where it lay.

I took care to feed the creature whenever I could, sneaking morsels of meat, both raw and cooked, down to his room every few days. It was after four weeks or so that I decided to move him up to my room. The move was a risky one, but bear in mind that he was the only friend I had, and it pained me to see him confined to the dark, cold rooms beneath Montcastle House. I had been given some freedom to rearrange the nursery room, so I asked Hugo to move a small wardrobe in from one of the guest bedrooms. Even with my few dresses hanging inside, there was room enough for the creature to hide. Far from being nervous, I felt comforted by the idea of him looking over me while I slept.

It was clear that he did not know how to speak – and had no inclination to learn – but that didn't stop me from talking to him during our secret liaisons. The day before making the move upstairs, I leaned in and whispered, 'Tomorrow you are coming to my room, to live with me. To the house upstairs. Tomorrow your new life begins.' I can't be sure that he heard me at all, or that he made sense of what I said, but I thought I detected an aura of satisfaction emanating from him the rest of that afternoon.

When the time came, the plan ran remarkably smoothly. Mrs Hardcliffe was in the habit of having Hugo drive her to the local church every Wednesday afternoon, whether for a service or some private assignation with the vicar was never disclosed to me. Once I'd heard the motor car crunch away up the drive, I waited for five minutes, playing solitaire with a set of cards on the bare floorboards of the nursery in an attempt to distract myself. Cook was still in the kitchen and I had spotted Agatha building a fire in the master bedroom, so there was no reason for my movements to be seen. When those five excruciatingly slow minutes had passed, I slipped out of my room and downstairs to the cellar door. Looking left and right there was nobody to be seen. Easing the door open as quietly as I could, I lit a candle I'd stolen earlier and descended into the world beneath.

The creature was heavier than I'd expected. It was only when I came to lift him, hoping to carry him silently back upstairs and into his new home, that my plan stumbled and threatened to come unstuck. I'm not particularly strong for my age, but I like to think that I have some vitality in me; that my muscles, while by no means toned, are still young and able. To my shock, though, I could barely lift him off the ground. He may have been small, but he weighed as much as a far, far larger man would, perhaps even several men. With a grunt I let him fall back to the floor. He turned that odd, featureless face of his towards me and gave me a look that I could not read.

In the end he took my hand and we ascended the steps together. His feet made a dull thudding noise against the stonework that did my nerves no good, but when we reached the corridor there was no one to be seen. I had half expected him to shy away from the daylight, after so many years below ground, but without eyes he appeared untroubled by it. His body gleamed in the sunlight as we padded along the corridors to the nursery room.

Slightly breathless with my own daring, I shut the door behind us and leaned against it. Now that he was here, in my room, I wasn't sure what to do with him. He would not be one for card games, of that I was certain. Any conversation would have to be one-sided in nature, too. For the first time I questioned what I was doing, and when I found no answers I felt the doubt begin to gnaw at my stomach.

The creature had his own ideas, though. He spent no more than a minute in the centre of the room before he seemed to take fright, and gradually shuffled towards the corner. When he reached it his hand brushed the cupboard I'd had brought in, and having found the handle he swiftly opened the door and stepped inside, shifting backwards until he discovered the corner. All that was needed was for me to rearrange my dresses around him, hiding him as best I could, and the plan was complete. From the middle of the room you would never have known he was there.

It may surprise you to learn that I had no immediate plans for him beyond the limited companionship he offered and my childish sense of adventure. It was enough at first to have done something so daring, to have this secret – this *mystery* – hidden in the recesses of my wardrobe. I thrilled at the hiddenness of it, the subterfuge for subterfuge's sake.

The memory of the lamb shank I had smuggled to him in the cellar stayed with me, however, and I would dwell upon it late at night, when the lights were out and I'd hear his footsteps as he explored our tiny kingdom in the blackness. The way those teeth had scored deep cuts into the bone. The hunger he had shown me.

Mrs Hardcliffe was in a particularly foul mood the day the idea came to me. When I spilled my milk on the tablecloth she rolled up her newspaper and thwacked me around the head with it, so hard that I felt uncommonly nauseous for several minutes after. Later in the day she called me over to her and held my hand in front of the fire, edging it closer and closer until I could feel the fine hairs on my wrist start to sizzle and wilt. When I cried out and pulled my hand free she simply laughed and called me a weak little girl. If her intention was to scare me into submission, it had the opposite effect. I left the room raging inside, swearing to have the last word.

I must confess, I had no idea it would work at all when I first conceived it, never mind work so strangely and so well. I simply looked about for a sharp instrument with which to wreak my revenge, and settled upon the most obvious weapon to hand. That I had little right to demand these services of the creature did not occur to me.

Late in the evening, when Agatha was busy turning down the beds for the night, I snuck into the hall and snatched one of Hardcliffe's gloves from the table there. Upstairs I became convinced that I should have taken the pair – nothing is more suspicious, after all, than a single glove left unattended – but it was too late to turn back. Once my door was closed, and I heard the footsteps retreat down the corridor, I slipped out of bed and opened the wardrobe door. The creature's cold hand burned as I guided him out into the room, but unlike my mistress's cruel tortures, the pain came as a comfort. Placing the glove in his hand, I leant down to bring my face close to his.

'Find her,' I said, my voice barely more than a whisper in the dark. 'Find the hand that filled this glove, and eat it.'

I lay awake in bed that night, listening to the creaking of the wooden floors, tossing and turning on a ship that had run aground. I thought at one point that I heard the latch click open, but after several minutes of silence I was forced to conclude that it was nothing more than the water pipes. I had hoped to hear the creature returning, but there was only the sound of the house groaning in its sleep. Perhaps he was gone for good. I had asked too much.

When I woke the next morning my first port of call was the wardrobe. Tugging aside the hanging dresses I saw him, knees pulled to his flawless chest, mouth open but slack. The lack of eyes made it difficult to tell when the creature was awake, but I had seen him in his moments of rest before.

Peering close, I tried to see some indication of the work he had done – a sliver of flesh between his needle teeth, a smear of red upon his chin – but there was nothing. I had to believe that he had failed, and I dressed with a heavy heart.

Mrs Hardcliffe did not come to breakfast as usual. Agatha served up my eggs and toast, poured a cup of tea and set my milk jug on the side. It was at lunchtime that I finally saw my captor, her face pale as Hugo helped her to her seat, and my breath caught in my throat. Where her hand should have been there was now only a stump. I had expected more from the wound, would have been cheered by gore and shredded muscles, but the damage was clean, a shining pink mound where her appendage should have been. It might have been an injury from several months earlier, already healing if not quite there yet – but I knew better. The creature had done his work well.

Naturally, doctors were called. From the village at first, but then further afield, as the medical profession tried to comprehend Mrs Hardcliffe's strange injuries. Yes, there were other wounds too. Slowly at first, but with increasing glee, I would send the creature out on these night-time forays, armed with a shoe, or a stocking, or a garter stolen from a bedside drawer. The thefts became easier as Hardcliffe was gradually eaten out of this world. Agatha managed only two weeks of this new nightmare, and most of the staff departed shortly after her. By the end it was only Hugo and I who kept company with the nub of gristle and flesh that used to be the lady of Montcastle House. Confined to her bed, she would be propped up by her faithful servant each morning, and tucked in at night. I do not know if he fed her, but imagine he must have. I would visit her sometimes, amusing myself by staring at those vacant, shell-shocked eyes, eyes which I am sure, by now, had seen more than any person should ever see.

As for the creature, I am ashamed to say that he grew fat and slow. Having survived for so many years on the slim pickings in the cellar room, his metabolism was not ready for this feast. Even his metallic hide began to lose its lustre. It seemed to me that the more he ate, the more he slept, and on several occasions I had to rouse him from a slumber to send him on his nocturnal visit. That he still departed with a sense of excitement and relish only confirms the famine he must have endured for all those years below ground.

I had to wake him from one of his naps on that final night. I had availed myself of one of Hardcliffe's riding hats during the afternoon, and once he had examined it I watched as he padded out of my room into the darkness. I was tempted to follow him and watch, but having witnessed the dull misery that sat behind his victim's eyes I cautioned myself against such folly. If curiosity might be so deadly, then I had no intention of being the cat.

Hugo found her the following morning, in quiet repose with her head resting upon the pillow, the top of it removed and the contents cleanly scooped out like a grapefruit. With nothing better to offer, the doctors eventually conceded that it must be some kind of flesh-eating bug, most likely introduced to the household when her cousin visited from India over a year before I arrived. That it made no sense didn't deter them from placing their signatures at the bottom of the autopsy. With no other explanation forthcoming it would simply have to do.

Those signatures allowed the estate to pass officially into the hands of her solicitor, and then, once the correct papers had been filed and the duties had been paid, it became mine. I allowed Hugo to stay, if only to keep the motor car running with the minimum of fuss. If he expected kinder treatment at the hands of his new employer, then he was disappointed.

The creature did not return that night, nor any night since. My suspicion is that he was finally sated and found his own way out of the house, back to the woods, or the burrows, or wherever it was that he once called home. I sometimes catch a shimmer of silver through the trees, or a metallic glint in the distance, and wonder if it might be him. In this age of motor cars and passenger planes, however, it might be anything at all.

RUT

When Sasha shouts for me I'm lying slumped between the barrels, a black bag of trash supporting my back. If she were to walk down the stairs to the cellar, into its dim, musty world, she would probably assume I had fallen. An ambulance would be called, my pulse would be taken. The doctors would shine their skinny torches into my eyes again, telling me to follow the light, follow the light.

I have not fallen. I'm simply resting, and daydreaming.

'Cedric? We need you up here, please. Tables to clear.'

My name is not Cedric. I should make that clear. They call me that, but it has never been my name. One of the customers, the barflies, called me it once, and the odour has followed me around. Thinking on it, it may have been Gary Chiltern. He's in here most nights, and every time he calls me 'Cedric' he spits it out, the taste of it unpleasant on his tongue. It would be in his nature to label me with something distasteful. I add it to the list of insults he has hurled my way.

'Cedric! Today, please?'

Unfurling from the floor, I push the trash bag against the wall, nudge the barrels aside. I may be scrawny, but I've hauled enough beer to have some strength in my shoulders, across the lean muscles of my chest. Once, I found a stuffed stag's head down here among the bar towels and paper napkins, still attached to its wooden mount. Holding it up in front of the mirror, I imagined myself as some beast of legend, a British cousin of the minotaur. My arms and legs are stick-thin, though, and this homespun myth crumbled. I lowered the stag's head and regarded myself with familiar self-loathing: my face narrow, my cheeks hollow.

I can't afford to lose this job. So I must stack my arms with lipstick-smeared glasses, wipe the sticky, stale residue from their tables. These are the acts that allow me to eke out an existence, to keep a roof above my head.

After the cool of the cellar, the bar is bright and busy, an eruption of sights and smells. Beer and disinfectant and cheap perfume. Once I can bear to open my eyes, I see Chiltern and his gang gathered at the far end of the bar. The one they call Popeye, his biceps grossly inflated to the size of a baby's head; Flynn, the skinniest of the bunch, his neck stained blue with dense inkwork that defies unravelling. Two of the ladies are with them: Chiltern's wife Melissa and Popeye's girlfriend, Mandy Dawes. My father knew hers, many years ago. We played in the same sandpits for a year or two. I have the photos, in the box I keep under my bed.

'Oi!' Chiltern shouts, raising his hands in the air. 'He finally surfaces! Where have you been, Cedric? Spitting in our beer, eh? Pissing on our peanuts?'

They laugh and I lower my face. This is the way it works around here.

Sasha is laughing with them behind the bar, her hand tight around the pumps as she pulls another round.

'Get lost down there, did you? The tables upstairs need clearing, and then there are glasses outside that need to come in. When you've done that, five needs changing too.'

She tosses me a cloth and I catch it, ignoring the droplets it spits in my face. My nostrils flare at the stink of the bleach.

'Yeah mate,' Chiltern says, 'my dogs are tied up out there too. Take them some water, will you? Nice one, Cedric. Chop-chop.'

Without a word, Sasha pushes a metal bowl along the bar towards me.

I hate Chiltern's dogs. I don't like dogs in general, but his in particular fill me with an unreasonable anxiety, a gut-churning fear. They're pit bulls, or something similar, the muscle packed tight beneath their skin, their eyes small and hard. One of them went for me once, sparking an outbreak of laughter around the bar, and they've never forgotten it. They know they own me, just like their master.

I take the bowl and half fill it at the tap. Night is starting to creep in as I push through the door, the air cold with the ghost of winter, but the daylight is stretching, grasping for the summer. There is a cut grass scent, fresh and green. At the edge of the light I can see the tall, dark mass of trees that mark the start of the woods. With shaking hands, I edge towards the two animals growling by the fence, my eyes cast down, watching the ripples in the bowl.

My dad grew up here, on the border of the common, the edge of the woods – and his father too. They walked the same paths between the tangled masses of brambles, rested their backs against the same ancient elms. Dad worked as a signalman on the railway line but he spent every spare moment outdoors, fetching wood for the fire, foraging berries and small, tart apples in the summer. I'm told that his father – my grandad – used to know the locations of all the badger setts, the best places to shoot rabbits or pigeons. I have this photo of him, faded now to shades of grey, his back against the thick trunk of an oak with a gun cocked over one arm, as casual as if it had grown out of the wood. I look at it sometimes and try to imagine how it must have been, to be at home in nature like that, to have lived in a time when the outdoors was part of your world. This place has changed since then. The world has turned. But the trees still hang on, reminding us of what once was, of the garden we have lost.

Dad used to tell me stories of the deer that roamed the woods, when he was a child. The way you'd steal glimpses of them through the trees, their tails bobbing white. His father would track them, following the trails of young bracken nibbled to the stem, picking up their scent of must and vinegar. Unlike the rabbits and the pigeons, he wouldn't kill them. They were the guardians of the woods, he said, the beating heart of the forest.

In all the time I have lived here, I have yet to see a single one.

I still live in the house that my grandfather owned, but only half of it is mine. My mum and dad sold off the first floor in the early eighties, to cover his debts. There is someone else living there now: a young man, constantly on the phone as he rushes out in his suit each morning. I can't remember his name. He floats above me, his feet never touching the ground.

*

At first the late-night walks were simply a way of clearing my head after a shift at the bar, winding down from the day. Then they became something more. Without knowing why, or how, I follow the paths and tracks as they weave through the trees, tracing a route that runs through me. It changes from night to night, but I can feel it tugging me this way and that, navigating via signs that I am barely aware of: an ancient elm, a clearing, a scent upon the wind. Sometimes I end up following a shallow ravine that runs through the forest floor, a dried-up remnant of some past flood, its bottom still boggy and damp. Other times I wander seemingly at random among the ferns and saplings. I imagine that these are the trails my father followed, and his father before him, that I'm walking the maps etched into my genes, but I have no proof. Maybe I'm just escaping from the twenty-first-century drudgery of my life. Maybe I'm just losing it again.

Sometimes I snatch a fistful of young bracken as I roam, the way my father taught me. These days the fiddlehead ferns are reserved for posh restaurants up in the city, but back in his day, in my grandad's day, people took sustenance where it was offered. The young shoots are almost sweet, bursting piney and green between my teeth. You have to take care, though. I remember him telling me they were poisonous in sufficient quantities, spiking your bloodstream with toxins that would make you hallucinate and, eventually, collapse. A little can keep you alive; too much will kill you.

Maybe it explains what I saw that day. It's almost four months ago now, maybe five – before the winter set in. A Sunday evening, the sunlight lancing through the trees, casting ever-changing patterns on the ground. My feet felt light, barely disturbing the scattered leaves. I remember stopping at a large oak, its bark scarred and pitted, a landscape in miniature. My gaze passed down the trunk, through the wooden valleys, to a hole that drilled between its roots. It wasn't a large hole, perhaps a foot across. Maybe a badger's sett, I thought. There were leaves and twigs scattered around its edges, a few dried brown cups left behind by last year's acorns. I could see only a few inches into the hole, then there was nothing but darkness.

It's tough to recall the exact sensations now. I remember my sight blurring, my skin hot and cold at once, as if I was about to be sick. The scent of the woods suddenly rose around me, rich and brown, the smell of compost and rotted leaves, of animal scat and decay. My head floated. The world spun.

Then, without warning, there was light.

Everything was washed in sunlight, the living radiance moving between the trees in waves and ripples, swelling and ebbing. I was almost blinded, not by the brightness, but by the variety. Colours and shades roiled before my eyes, and I wondered if this was it – if I was about to die. The ghost of the bracken rose in my throat, and I tasted my father's warning.

And then I saw him. Walking through the trees thirty, forty feet from me, a colossal man, as tall as some of the trunks that swayed apart to allow his passage. As he stalked in and out of the shade he would vanish from sight, only to re-emerge into the sunlight, a glimpse of muscle here, of branching antler there. Given my condition I couldn't be certain that I wasn't imagining him – but there was the smell too, a ripe stink of animal and man, sweat mingled with a vinegary musk and a clinging, damp odour like moss. His torso was bare, a loincloth of sorts around his waist. But from his shoulders upwards the skin turned to pelt, dark and shaggy, topped by a giant stag's head, antlers branching to the sky.

He turned to face me and his mouth opened in a bellow of challenge.

In that moment, I passed out.

*

Chiltern and his gang are the last to leave. They let the door swing shut with a crash, cutting Gary off as he says something about taking the dogs for a walk, letting them sniff their way around the woods. There's a whoop of laughter from one of them – Flynn, I think – then the mutter of their voices fades. The night falls silent.

'Right,' Sasha says, the glasses rattling as she loads them into the washer, 'let's get this place closed. All the tables upstairs need wiping, I'll take the bar. I want to get out before midnight.'

I don't mind closing time. Without the people cluttering it, the bar feels spacious, calm. The tables are all real wood, knotted and lined. They were probably imported from somewhere north of here – Scotland, the Russian steppes – but they bring me closer to the trees. There is nature here, even if it isn't ours.

Someone has left a woollen jumper under one of the tables. Light blue, a handful of sky. I consider keeping it, taking it for my own. I can barely afford to buy clothes these days, and the nights are still cold, the winter clinging on in the small hours of the morning. I tell myself that there is nothing wrong with foraging to survive. But I place it behind the bar, tucked into the cubby we use for lost property, as Sasha does the final checks on the till. They'll come asking for it tomorrow, I'm sure.

Sasha barely looks at me as she locks up. When she's done, she glances over her shoulder with a muttered 'See you tomorrow'. Then she's gone, walking quickly up the well-lit path to the Cranstone Estate, her hands pushed deep into her pockets.

I stand for a moment, filling my nostrils with the cool air. Then I walk towards the woods.

*

Tonight, my path is almost straight. I can feel the thread leading me somewhere, although I don't know where. The trees are growing closer here, the trunks wider, and I am aware, somehow, that I am moving nearer to the heart of the woods. Something stirs in me, raw and primeval. Without thinking, my hand snaps the tightly-curled head off a fern and I rub it between finger and thumb as I walk. Touch my fingers to my tongue for just a hint of a taste. The dry leaves whisper beneath my feet but otherwise everything is still, the air lying cold and heavy.

Then I hear voices.

They are too distant to make out what is being said, but they are undoubtedly human. My pace automatically slows, my feet treading cautiously. It must be gone midnight. I have never met anyone out here during my night walks before, and the possibility worries me. There has always been a purity to the night-time forest, a silence that's as timeless as it is rooted in the moment. Usually I can daydream that the modern world has yet to happen. But tonight, something is wrong. It's as I creep closer that I make out Gary Chiltern's voice. I know it too well for there to be any doubt. He's laughing, and the sound triggers a fear in me that prickles across my scalp. The Chilterns of this world do not belong here.

There's another voice, a woman's. I assume it's Melissa's at first, but I quickly realise that it's different, a touch higher, more nasal. I can't place it, so I shuffle forward, trying to make them out. Chiltern I can see, the heavy bulk of him pushing somebody up against the trunk of a tree. His hands move across her and she laughs too. He steps to one side, adjusting his stance, and I glimpse her face in the shadows. Not Melissa, then. It's Mandy – Mandy Dawes, Popeye's girl. The girl I used to share a sandpit with, all those many years ago. Her skirt has ridden up around her waist, and as I watch, Chiltern's rough, unsubtle hand pushes up beneath its folds. His other hand tugs at his belt and then his buttocks are bared, two pale moons in the darkness, and she laughs that laugh again, her own hands helping him. There's a grunt that can only be Chiltern's, a deep, animal sound, and Mandy gasps.

Something in me senses the danger of what I'm seeing and I start to back away, retreating into the densest part of the woods. But my heel catches a dry stick, and with a sharp *crack* it announces its presence – and mine – to the night air. Mandy's hands immediately move to smooth down her skirt. Chiltern tugs up his jeans as his head snaps in my direction. I try to remain still, my breath snagged in my throat.

'Is there someone out there, Gary? Did you hear it?'

Chiltern mutters something about peeping toms that I can't quite hear. His back is to me as he moves around the trunk, bending low to the ground, his hands busy as they loosen a knot.

'Don't worry, love,' he says, his voice finding a way to me through the undergrowth. 'The boys will sniff him out.'

Then, black bullets, the two dogs shoot out from behind the tree and I'm running, crashing through the bracken and the brambles, their thorns tearing at my coat. I can hear barking behind me but I have no clue how close they are, whether they have found my scent. I have to assume the worst. Wherever I am, there's no way I can make it back home from here, so I let my instincts guide me. The stink of sweat rises from my body and I wonder if I have always smelled like this; if my nose has become more acute, or if the fear has made me reek. Either way, it seems unfeasible that the dogs will not sniff it out.

My calves are stiffening but I hurtle on as best I can, branches whipping my face. The barking sounds close behind me now, the snaps and cracks as twin bodies careen through the undergrowth. Without knowing how, I have found the shallow ravine again and I follow its course, my feet sticking in the boggy ground as I run. Perhaps on some level I hope this will hide my scent, but all I feel is the fear pumping through me, the need to flee, fast, to put some space between me and my pursuers.

And then, to hide. The thought comes to me unbidden. I can't outrun them, I can't make it home. So I must hide, and hide well. Somewhere they won't find me, or won't be able to follow. Somewhere safe.

The ravine pushes uphill for a short time, and as it does I think I hear the barks falling behind. When I reach the top of the incline the ground levels out, but in front of me lies a massive, sprawling bramble patch, at least twenty feet wide, its thorny tangle dense and unwelcoming. The dogs will not dare to follow me in there, I think. Dropping to my knees, I find a low tunnel beneath the massed branches, where a fox or maybe a badger has made its path. I push my nose to the ground. My back catches on the thorns as I wriggle inside, so I drop even lower, my belly in the dirt, pulling myself forward with my hands. Something scratches the back of my neck but I carry on, inch by inch, until I must be at least seven or eight feet inside the bramble patch. I lift my head tentatively and nothing pricks it, nothing tugs at my back. Slowly, cautiously, I pull myself up into a crouch.

The dogs are circling outside. I can hear them testing the edges of the thicket, the restless padding of their paws on the leaves. There's a growl from my left, so low I feel it more than hear it. A sudden warmth in my groin and I realise that I've wet myself, the sharp stink of piss mixing with my sweat as it stabs at my nostrils. I curl my fists and squeeze closed my eyes.

There's silence for a second, two, three – as if the wind has dropped suddenly, the woods quiet and still, everything holding its breath. Then, to my surprise, I hear a whimper of fear to my left, followed by an echoed whimper straight ahead. Both dogs are simpering now, high-pitched and submissive. For the first time, the fear I sense is not my own. I hear a loud creak, like a tree uprooting itself, then a soft, wet *thud*. The animal noises stop and there is a second *thud*, even louder than the first, underlined by a sharp *crack*. Then it's quiet again.

I wait for what feels like a minute or two, although it may be longer. Time has concertinaed with the hormones fizzing through my blood. When it's clear that the dogs have gone, I drop to my belly once again, the warmth in my crotch now cold against the earth, and wriggle back through the bramble tunnel.

The first animal is waiting for me when I emerge. One of Chiltern's pit bulls, lying black and heavy on the ground. Its head is unnaturally flattened on the side facing me, and as I watch I see lines of crimson starting to seep through the fur, joining together and pooling as its blood drips onto the forest floor. Looking closer, its hind legs bend at unnatural angles, snapped in at least three places.

The second pit bull is behind it, hauled into sight as I rise to my feet. It's suspended a good ten feet off the ground, the broken branch of an oak piercing its belly and emerging through the shattered ribcage on the other side.

When I spot what I believe to be its intestines swinging from the branch I'm finally sick, the contents of my stomach forcing their way out without warning. I'm sick again and I spit, washing the acidic aftertaste from my mouth. It's then that I see him. He's barely visible between the trees: a large, dark mass in the shadows. A breeze rustles the leaves and moonlight falls upon a giant chest, muscles speckled with patches of velvet. Antlers branch into the canopy overhead, the heat of his breath shimmering about his nostrils. If I hadn't already soiled myself I would be doing so now, but instead I shiver in my wet pants, my stomach hollow and plummeting. My thighs are already stiffening with the burn; I don't know if I can manage another chase. Without warning he bellows, a roar as loud as any bear's, guttural and wild.

Then he pushes his way back through the woods, merging into the shadowy undergrowth, leaving me standing in my piss and my vomit and the rapidly spreading pool of blood, while all around me the trees whisper to the dark.

AFTER THE RESERVOIR

He snags his school jumper on the fence as he climbs, and when he drops into the grass beneath he hears it rip. Shrugging the bag from his shoulder, he twists his arm back, trying to see. There's a hole there, but no blood. Must just be a tear. His mum would kill him, but that doesn't matter now.

There's a cool wind blowing off the water as Martin scrambles down the slope, his feet occasionally sliding out from beneath him. He feels as if he is surfing. The grass on this side is flattened down, the wind pressing it back against the earth, but on the far bank he can see it swaying and flowing in waves, like a living thing. He's so distracted that he slips, travelling the rest of the way down on his butt. He smiles at the ripe green stain smeared across his trousers.

He has a vague idea of where he's going. He's been here before, once, with Mike and Stu. They were daring each other, pretending to explore the wilds. They had found the foundation of an old concrete building, now nothing more than a ten-foot-square block set into the ground, rusted spikes of unknown purpose jutting from the middle. Stu said it used to be the base for an anti-aircraft gun, the last defence against an invasion from the skies, but they all knew he was talking shit. Nobody defends a reservoir in the back end of nowhere from anything, least of all enemy invasion. When he asked his dad he'd said that it used to be a pumping station, but then he'd looked at him that way he did, his eyes dark and dead, and he'd known not to say any more. Whatever it was, it wasn't worth risking a beating for.

He's comforted to see that the concrete is still there, one corner greened with algae where the rainwater has sat and stagnated. There's a crack he didn't notice before, something forcing its way through the solid foundations a fraction of an inch at a time, a green bud just starting to rise from the black scar. One day, he imagines, this will all be green. Caught in the nettles behind it is a ball of blue plastic sheeting, and he fishes it out with care, making sure not to touch the leaves. It looks mostly intact, so he folds it the best he can and stows it in his bag. It's not heavy, but the bulk pushes against his spine as if there's somebody behind him.

Standing with his feet on the concrete he can see the small copse close to the reservoir's edge, seven or eight trees clustered together near to the water. He'd noted it that first time, with Mike and Stu, and remembers thinking that it would make a good place for a camp. It should be sheltered from the wind a little, and out of sight. They would never think to look for him down there. If he's lucky, he can disappear.

There's no path around this end of the water, so he picks up a stick and swishes it back and forth in front of him, cutting through the weeds as he forces his way down. A patch of thistles refuses to yield before his makeshift scythe, and they scratch at his legs as he wades through them, even through his trousers. He doesn't mind the pain, though. It's a good kind of pain, the kind that reminds him he's alive. The next patch, he doesn't even bother with the stick, just walks through them, grinning as they claw at his legs.

The copse is smaller than he'd thought. The trees had looked larger from a distance, but close up they're not much more than saplings. The largest, a birch, he can almost stretch his hands around its trunk. They'll do, though. He finds a couple of branches and makes short work of lashing them together, using the string he took from Mum's kitchen. When he comes to drape the blue plastic sheeting over the top he's pleased to find that it's a good fit. There's an L-shaped tear at one end but he hopes it isn't large enough to let the rain in. If it does, he'll have to rethink.

The sun is starting to set as he sits on the grass and chews on a Snickers bar. He wishes he'd brought something more filling, but he wasn't thinking straight. It seemed better just to go. He'd had the presence of mind to raid his dad's drinks cabinet, though, and there are five small bottles clinking against each other in the bottom of his rucksack. He knows he'd get a beating for that for sure, and the thought makes him smile. There's no going back now. Maybe that was why he did it.

He'd thought they were all vodka, but one says 'Jose Cuervo' on the label. He's never drunk tequila before, but Stu once told a story about how his brother got so drunk on it that he puked in his own shoe. He decides to leave that one till last. The tiny metal cap on one of the vodka bottles twists off with a satisfying crackle, and as he lifts it to his lips the smell stings his eyes. There's a burn as he swallows, but he manages not to cough. A man can take his liquor. His stomach gurgles briefly, wondering whether it should keep this meagre meal down, but by the third or fourth sip it settles into numb acceptance. Martin feels a little dizzy, and he likes it.

As the sun drops lower, brushing the horizon, he opens the second bottle, supping at it more eagerly. The wind has picked up and whistles through the grass, the noise grating against his nerves, fingernails down a blackboard. He wonders if it's the grass that's causing it, or another concrete structure somewhere, funnelling the breeze. Tomorrow he'll explore, see what he can find.

It's as the darkness falls that he begins to feel afraid. He's never been one to shy away from ghost stories; they always struck him as something for kids, or the simple-minded, like Hughey Green who collected the trolleys at Tesco's. He'd seen Hughey down here at the reservoir more than once, staring vacantly at the water. Ghosts and hauntings weren't real, any more than fairy godmothers were real, or unicorns. *If you really want to be scared*, he'd say, whenever anyone talked about the latest horror they'd watched on Sky, *you should come round my place when my dad gets back from the pub.* He hadn't been joking, but people laughed anyway.

Now that he's outside, surrounded by real darkness, real wilderness, it all feels different. The whistling ebbs and flows, rising in volume until he convinces himself it's a shriek of anger, the cry of something supernatural among the grass and weeds; then it fades again, like it's moving away, and he allows himself a breath. It's getting darker than he's seen before, now that he's away from the lights and the traffic, and he shuffles backwards, so he's sitting under the protection of his makeshift bivouac. The shelter it offers is less substantial than he'd hoped. He starts as he hears an animal noise close by, partway between a whinny and a bark. He tells himself that the sound carries out here, across the water. Still, he holds tight to his stick.

It's as he sips at the fourth bottle of vodka, his last, that the sounds change. It's subtle at first, a slight shift in timbre that he barely registers. But the shift in his mood is more marked, the haunted feeling fading away as the alcohol burns through his blood, and being replaced by – what? His thoughts are muddled, and he struggles to define it, but the fear has gone and in its place there is something close to awe, or wonder. As his imagination grips hold of this it occurs to him that the whistling now sounds less like a ghost than it does a vast emptiness, a timeless nothing that stretches farther than he can comprehend. He imagines it's what it sounds like to be drifting in space, the not-quite-silence of the billions of miles of vastness between the planets.

He's not sure when the lights come. He has passed into a tipsy reverie, so it might be past midnight or only minutes after the sun has fallen. At first he thinks they have found him. They must be searching, his mother would have called the police as soon as she noticed he wasn't in his room. There's one light at first, small and faint, like a distant torch, then it's joined by three others, moving and jostling each other as if they're making their way down the far bank. He considers hiding, but it seems pointless, childish even. They either find him or they don't. There's little he can do about it.

After several minutes of watching the lights haven't grown any larger, however, and Martin realises that the direction is wrong too. If they were coming down the slope he'd see them off to his left, but these are straight ahead. They're close, not small because they're at a distance, but actually no bigger than a marble. They could be reflections on the surface of the reservoir, he supposes. But there is no sign of a source, nowhere nearby they could be reflected from. Standing woozily, his head grazing the plastic sheet above, he wanders down to the water's edge to take a better look.

As he stands on the bank, his toes just touching the water, Martin can see whatever it is more clearly. It's a few feet below the surface, partially obscured by the murky waters but still visible. Four lights – no, five – glowing with a blue fire that defies explanation. They might be some kind of bioluminescent fish, but if so he has heard of nothing of the sort before. Not around here. There's a sound too, a whispering susurrus that he feels as much as he hears, his skin prickling with it as it surrounds him. And a smell. He can't quite define it, but it reminds him of the chlorine at the council pool, the cold sting of the TCP his mum dabs onto his cuts. Without knowing why, he shivers. His eyes do not leave the lights.

They rise slowly, almost imperceptibly, growing larger in tiny, immeasurable increments as whatever it is drifts to the surface. There are more of them now, perhaps twenty, some deeper than others as they drift in the water. His skin starts to ache with the vibrations in the air. His teeth itch. He exists in a bubble of light, the darkness beyond it forgotten, nothing more than a formless vacuum.

Without thinking what he's doing, Martin kneels down in the mud. He stretches out his arm and dips his hand into the water.

The change is instant. The whispering vanishes, replaced by a deep vibration, as if something is resonating beneath the water's surface. The lights are still there but they're also not there, they were and will be and never have been, a tiny ripple in an endless expanse. He can't explain it, but Martin no longer exists. Not in the way he did before, not as a person. He has no hand, he has no arm; there is no water, no reservoir, no England. It is still there, but only a trace, a wisp of something that may once have been, or one day will be.

As he grapples with the strangeness of it, he becomes aware of something there with him. Not a creature, but an awareness; an intelligence that is both formless and vast. It doesn't speak, not in any way that Martin can recognise, it's simply there, and the knowledge comes to him that whatever this is – this being, this consciousness – it has been here longer than the people, longer even than the trees, or the rocks. It seems immeasurably old, so old that the word no longer applies, not in any real sense. Time does not exist for it; or if it does, then it is little more than a distraction. Today, yesterday, tomorrow, a thousand years from now – they are all the same. It simply is.

Then it's gone. Just like that, with no warning or sign, no great flash of revelation, its presence vanishes. Martin is back at the reservoir, his hand cold in the water, his knees wet against the bank. The wind still whistles through the grass, through the concrete ruins, but it is simply the wind now, nothing more. The night is black, illuminated only by a sliver of moon visible through the clouds.

He stays like that for several minutes, remembering how to breathe, feeling the steady pulse of his heart. Then Martin rocks back onto the grass and sits there, staring out across the waters of the reservoir, his hand drying slowly in the cool night air. He will still be sitting there when they find him the next morning. They will take him to A&E and have him checked for hypothermia, keep him in for observation for forty-eight hours, fill him with soup and bread and pasta. His mum will worry over him, her hand on his forehead at least once an hour; his dad will shout at him when they get him home, beat him for the trouble he's caused until his back and legs are bruised and numb. But Martin will simply stare, and stare, and none of this will seem real; not today, not tomorrow, not forever.

STATIC RITUAL
(WITH DAN CARPENTER)

When the package was delivered, Eliot abandoned it on the porch for a week. He passed it each morning on his way to work, and again in the evening, the dimming light drowning it in shadows. He hoped that someone might steal it, or that it would otherwise disappear; scavenged by racoons, vanishing into the ether.

Over the weekend, he found himself looking at the brown paper with increasing frequency. When he returned to the office on Monday, he asked Jules where they stored all the old hardware, the obsolete technology. He knew they wouldn't have thrown it away. She pointed him to a cupboard, and among the Minidiscs and handheld dictation machines he discovered a VHS player. A JVC Videostar, the top-loading model, panelled with fake-wood laminate that had cracked and peeled at the edges. The tape cover and loading tray were missing, but he thought it would work. At the end of his shift he walked out with it under his arm.

The package still lingered on his porch when he arrived home. The address was written in a childish squiggle, clumped in one corner. The back was sealed with a single, grimy strip of masking tape, the ends beginning to curl. Carrying it inside, he plugged the player in and slid a scissor blade across one end of the tape.

Even as he upended it, he hoped he was mistaken. Then the video cassette clattered onto the table. The labels were gone, only a few remnants remaining. It looked as if someone had scratched them off with their nails. Over these scraps a single sticker had been plastered at an angle, as if it was an afterthought, the number 5 written on it in thick, black pen.

Eliot stared at the cassette for a moment, then at the VCR, and finally at the flat-screen TV he had connected it to. He stood and grabbed a beer from the fridge, sat back down. After a few minutes the can burned cold against his palm and he took a deep breath, as if he was about to throw himself from a great height. If he waited any longer he thought he might be sick.

The tape slotted easily into the top of the machine, despite the lack of a loading tray. There was a loud clunk as it locked into place and the spindles lurched. He could see the cogs turning inside, the black tape spooling from one side to the other with a barely audible hiss. He drained most of the beer in a single gulp, then he watched.

A black screen, dirt caught on the negative flickering across every few frames. The blackness. A space between the horrors. You brace yourself for what is to come, knowing it will be her. Knowing she will be in that room again.

A white line races up the screen, interference dashes across like stars. Then she appears. Just for a few frames, then gone again, but it's enough for you. You know her curled blonde hair, the black dress, like a movie star from the fifties. Once again, behind her, curtains billow in from a gentle evening breeze. A deep, arresting blue sky. You blink and her red lipstick echoes across your vision. Then she returns; this time, standing with her back to you, looking out over the balcony. The blue sky darker now. A bleached moon rising beyond whatever city she is in. In the distance, an enormous mountain range straddles the horizon. A harsh cut, and then she's lying on the bed, writhing. Static racing across the screen. The orange hue of lit candles surrounds her. In the background, the mountains bristle in the breeze. Hundreds of trees, tiny like the hairs on the legs of spiders, catch the wind and ripple. The woman on the bed continues. Is she laughing, or straining?

Another cut. The sunlight pours into the room. Where is she? Nowhere to be seen, but for the first time, sound shoots through the speakers, a shower running. The water, arrestingly loud, straining your speakers. The camera seems to be static, but there's a telltale disjointedness, a lopsided view of the bathroom door, ajar. Steam drifts from the gap. Jolting to the side, the camera lurches towards the door. Closer and closer and then—

Another cut. Outside again, shot from the balcony. The sky black and huge, an orange hue at the top. It's as though the horizon has been hoisted up, or the mountains that once lay calm just beyond the balcony have shifted, lifted themselves. You move yourself closer to the screen, the way you did all those years ago. The image fills your whole vision. You spill into it. Staring at the blackness which has become the horizon. Why does it remind you so much of that first video? Who is filming this?

The blackness moves, the mountains shift and unfurl. They block the moon and blacken the sky. They are not mountains. Some thing lies across the horizon. An enormous horror you can't understand. As it rises and blots out the light beyond the water you catch your reflection in its flesh.

*

It was all Eliot could do to press one jittering fingertip against the stop button, watch the screen retreat into black. The machine clicked, whirred, and fell silent. He reached for his beer and swallowed the dregs, bitter at the back of his throat.

When his hands were calm, he reached out and pressed rewind.

<u>2007</u>

It was after Cheryl threw him out that he found the package. Eliot was so disoriented by the one-bedroom apartment, the sudden lack of emotional closeness, that he didn't register it at first. It sat in a cardboard box for several weeks, between a stack of paperback thrillers and a half-full CD rack. She had taken the lighter stuff, leaving him with Papa Roach and a couple of OutKast albums. He assumed the package was empty, a leftover shell from his former life.

Because of this, he opened it casually, expecting to throw it away. He was midway through a mug of coffee and a slice of toast. Anticipating nothing inside, the tape came as a shock. He still had a few VHS cassettes somewhere among the boxes, he still knew what this was, but he barely watched them. It was all discs now, the shiny, silver efficiency of the new age. As soon as he touched it the plastic struck him as clunky and primitive, relying on the mechanical physicality of cogs and wheels. His VHS player may have a digital display, but its innards were only a generation away from clockwork. Whenever he used it he found himself hoping for a mechanical cuckoo to pop out.

He didn't remember. Not at first. Then he saw the small, square label on the plastic, the number 4 inscribed in crude, black ink.

The coffee sat cold in the mug. The toast turned dry and stale.

He had to watch it, of course. There was something irresistible about knowing that the images were there, beneath his fingertips, magnetic echoes seared onto yard after yard of tape. He may not have been able to run his fingers over them, but they were as real as his pre-loved couch, the cheap box spring on his bed. A presence in the room. How could he help but look?

When the cassette clunked into position, nothing happened. The TV screen remained blank. It took him a moment to realise that he hadn't connected the player at the back of the set, the obsolete technology sitting low on his list of priorities. When he eventually found the right hole and slid the connector in, the image and sound jolted to life, and his breath caught in his throat.

*

The camera starts in the doorway of an apartment. The cream walls dashed with porcelain mosaic, creating patterns that could almost be letters or words, if they were written in any language you recognise. It moves slowly, almost floating down the hall. It has been eighteen years since the first one, so why not take your time, you think. The unseen operator (in more ways than one, you recall), continues down the corridor, passing a number of closed doors, until it reaches a lounge. A long couch rests alongside a wall, facing towards a set of French windows. Beyond that, a balcony, teeming with sunlight. In the distance, a mountain range, rich with greenery. Where is this? You don't recognise it as being anywhere near you, and there are no landmarks you can see.

There is a judder, and a handful of upside-down frames flicker past.
Where's the woman? *you think.* What happened to her?
The frame becomes bleached, washed out. Then it blacks out altogether. When

158 | Dan Coxon

it returns, the camera no longer lingers where it did. Instead, it is in a bedroom. Unlit candles have been placed around the bed and the curtains have been drawn, letting a thin sliver of light through, bisecting the room.

A figure enters from behind the camera, walking into frame, briefly blocking it. The screen goes black as he passes by, but it is unlike the blackness of a shadow passing in front of the image. This is closer to the blackness of a blank tape. Another absence. The figure moves past the camera and approaches the bed. He – and it is almost definitely a he, despite his back being towards the camera – stands at the foot of the bed. He's dressed in a long cloak, hood up. Resting his arms at his sides, he reveals a knife. He raises it in the air and carves out shapes. As he does, tiny scratches notch themselves into the frame of the video. Patterns that do not appear to be in any language. Shapes that hold no meaning.

The frame jitters and breaks, then the screen goes black once more.

*

Eliot slumped into the couch, his breathing ragged. It was back, then. It was almost comforting to know that there was still a constant in his life. Almost, but not quite. There had to be a meaning to it all, a purpose hidden in the magnetic code, but it was lost on him. Everything was lost, everything was hidden.

He knew he had to watch it again. He also knew that he would watch it every night for the next week, entranced by the strange images, the rawness, the suggested acts of unseen violence. It had happened before, so it would happen again. The tape played from spool to spool, over and over.

He reached out and pressed rewind.

<u>2001</u>

At first, he assumed it was hers. Cheryl's; his wife's. He still hadn't grown used to calling her that, even though the wedding was back in July. It sounded so grown-up. In his head, he was still a kid.

The house – their house – was jumbled with the fallout of two single lives, thrown together by chance, by love. There were duplicates of some of the albums – Matchbox Twenty, No Doubt – and even more of the videos. For some reason, they now owned three copies of *Men in Black*. Eliot meant to buy racks for them, to replace the cardboard boxes, but it was low enough on the list of priorities that it kept getting delayed. Cheryl claimed to hate his untidy ways, but she was just as bad. Between them, it was a miracle they could see the carpet.

It was little wonder, then, that he didn't recognise the cassette at first. Half the contents of the house were unfamiliar. It was only while searching for his copy of *Independence Day* that he lifted the black VHS cassette and glanced at the spine, wondering where the box had gone.

There was only one label, and it bore the number 3.

Without thinking, Eliot sat down where he was, something plastic crunching beneath his weight. He stared at the cassette in his hand as if appraising it, weighing the contents of the tape contained inside. The black plastic casing felt slightly sticky to the touch, and he wiped his hand on the leg of his jeans. Finally, he remembered to breathe.

When the tape clunked into the machine it sounded louder than normal, the usual susurration underpinned by a high-pitched whine. He sat cross-legged in the chaos of his new, married life, and watched the images crackle across the convex screen.

*

This time you can see her clearly. It appears at first glance to be a photograph. The blonde hair, bouffant and curled. The red lipstick. Just a still image of some actress. But then she curls a forced smile. You feel embarrassed, as though you have intruded on her. She doesn't seem to want the camera in her face. Her eyes flit about the screen, looking everywhere except down the lens. You squirm in your seat, try to look away, but you can't. You're captivated. By the tape, by her. You think back to that single word you heard all those years ago. Had it been her voice? Her blurred outline? You squint. It could very easily have been her. How old is this video?

The image flickers for a few broken frames, then returns to her. The camera is behind her now as she looks in a mirror. Something doesn't seem right about it, and you watch as an arm reaches into frame and helps apply make-up to her face. As she stares into the mirror you find a sadness within her, and a resignation too.

But there is something else that feels wrong. Something you can't put your finger on. The camera lingers in the room. You look around, trying to find details, but there are none. The walls are plain. The mirror reflects nothing but the woman. Nothing but the woman. The angle that the camera has found, the way it's placed. It's impossible. The camera should be there. Should be reflected too. But there is no camera. No cameraman. How can that be?

The image jolts and the black screen returns.

*

The whining noise intensified, and his stomach flipped as there was a sudden snap and a fluttering from the player. Then it stopped. When he pressed eject it spat the cassette out, its entrails spilling from the back. He pulled handful after handful of tape from the machine, until it seemed as if there could not be any more. He ended up with a pile almost as big as the TV itself.

Eliot spent the afternoon winding the tape back onto the spools by hand, ironing out the creases between his palms. He didn't know whether it would work or not, but he had to see more, had to find out what happened next. One section of the tape was scrunched and ripped beyond repair, so he cut it out with a razor blade and spliced the ends together. It might not hold, and whatever was on that section had been lost, but it was better than nothing. Eventually, not trusting the machine, he wound it all back from right to left, keeping the tape as tight as he could, forcing time to move backwards.

The tape tension was poor, and the image fluttered on the screen, but it was there. He leant forward to get closer to the screen. Watched, entranced.

1995

It was a quiet Sunday afternoon in the store. Eliot spent most of his day reading textbooks, making notes. He would be back at college in two weeks, and he needed to improve his grades if he was to stay on. For lunch he microwaved a burrito, but otherwise his head was between the pages; reading, writing, revising.

It was almost six o'clock before he decided that he deserved a break. The store closed at eight, so he had two hours – long enough for a movie. The shelves were stacked with the latest releases, row upon row of *The Mask* and *Speed*, *The Lion King* and *The Shawshank Redemption*. He felt like something older tonight, though. Something stranger. Mark, the owner, was very particular about what they screened, so he knew it should be family-friendly. Not a cartoon, though. He couldn't stand cute.

After browsing the Drama shelves for a minute, he settled on an old black-and-white movie, *Night of the Hunter*. He'd heard of it, never seen it. Robert Mitchum straddled the cover, the words 'Love' and 'Hate' tattooed on his knuckles. That was enough to draw him in. The blurb said something about a serial killer, but it was from the fifties, so he assumed it should be okay. If anyone complained, he'd plead ignorance.

When he clicked open the case, however, the cassette had no label. No, that wasn't exactly true – there was a small, handwritten label, with the number 2 scrawled on it with a Sharpie. The label reminded him of something, although he couldn't say what. If it was *Night of the Hunter*, then someone had defaced it. He'd have to fill out a damage report (Mark was a stickler for those too); failing that, it would be a lost tape form. Either way, there was paperwork.

Sighing, he slotted it into the player. The small TV suspended above the counter crackled.

*

It is, at first glance, just a blank tape. A fuzzy blackness fills the screen and remains static for a few minutes. You push fast forward on the remote. Nothing but blackness, punctured with rising white lines. Then, a flash of colour, and gone again. You stop the tape and rewind. The flash of colour again. You press hard on the pause button, fracturing the screen between frames. It flickers. That black nothing and then, something blurred. An image, out of focus. This is no blank tape. You press play and then immediately pause again, trying to stop it perfectly on the frame. It remains out of focus, but, squinting your eyes, you can make out a figure. A woman, possibly? There's an outline of a figure that could be seen to be a person, but it's barely there. So why a woman? Why has that come to you so easily?

You rewind the tape back to the start and push play, in case you missed anything else. Wherever this thing came from, it feels somehow different.

The blank screen again. Nothing and nothing. But there is something, you know you felt something. Then you hear it. The whirr of the video player is being drowned out. Some kind of white noise being emitted by the tape itself. You edge closer to the screen, place your ear on the speaker. It's there. Barely noticeable. And then, it speaks.

It says one word: Help.

1989

Eliot didn't realise it, but he was lucky to get the job at the video store. He was only sixteen, so they shouldn't have hired him at all, but he managed a good interview and the owner needed someone who could start straight away. Their weekend guy had gone AWOL, vanished from the face of the earth – or from town, at least. There were rumours about drug deals, illicit trades under the counter at night. Eliot may have been young, but at least there was no risk of that.

He settled in well. He was still at that age when everything came naturally; he never questioned the luck that fell into his lap. It seemed the most normal thing in the world to be sitting on a stool behind the counter, checking that the tapes were rewound when they were returned, logging out new rentals on the customers' membership cards. Brad and Mike dropped by and tried to take out *The Serpent and the Rainbow*, but they were happy enough to leave with *Beetlejuice*. They'd heard there was a scene where a woman ripped her own face off.

It was while processing the previous night's returns that he came across the cassette. It looked the same as all the others, but it had no label.

Someone had stuck a sticker on the side with the number 1 on it, but that was all – no title, no rating, nothing. Without really thinking, he slotted it into the machine.

*

A black screen stares at you. You can see your own face in the glass. Some moron went and dropped the wrong tape off, you think. Or this is all just some lame kind of joke. You pick up the remote and speed through the remaining videotape. Nothing. When you hit play again it's just more of the same. Just the escaped air hiss of nothing. But there is something about the tape. You rewind it and play it again from the beginning. Some part of you has the strangest of thoughts when you press play the second time. That somehow it will be different. That somehow the video will change. It's the same the third time, and the fourth. But something keeps you coming back. You play it a fifth time, and this time you don't skip ahead or look away. You stare unblinking at the screen. Your expression stares back at you, a curious concentration on your face.

Eventually, you focus on the screen itself, and can no longer see your reflection. It's completely blank. A total absence. But there is something there, you can feel it. A presence lurking in the video somewhere. You reach out and touch the screen, recoiling slightly at the prick of the static shock. The crackle of electricity against your hand makes the hairs on your fingers stand on end, but you aren't thinking about that. Instead, you're looking at the curve of the screen, at the blackness within, imagining that you're stroking some creature. Ruffling its fur. You run your hand up the screen until you reach the very tip of it.

The video stops.

You play it another ten times that night, after the store has closed. The door is locked, the lights are switched off. You stay watching the screen for a long, long time.

══ALL THE LETTERS IN HIS VAN ══

Through the woods and down the hill and over the tracks we come to a sign. It is bolted to a crumbling drystone wall, the letters obscured by moss and mildew, and what appears to be sheep shit. We can read the letters G-R-E-E-N-D— before they disappear entirely. It should be a sign, that sign.

'Green *something* then,' Debbie says. 'Sounds nice. Should we stop?'

Our feet are aching, our packs weigh heavy on our backs. Rainwater has seeped through my jacket, leaving my neck and shoulders cold and damp. We are lost and we need to rest for the night. Our phones are off the grid. It is no decision at all.

Walking through the village neither of us mentions the emptiness. It doesn't occur to either of us to ask where the inhabitants of all these cottages are, why the streets are empty of children, or pets, or cars. Everything looks normal. Photos are propped on window ledges. Welcome mats call out to our muddied boots. Everything is perfect and yet nothing makes sense.

'Seems quiet,' I say. 'No kids.'

Debbie says nothing. Four miscarriages in the last three years will do that to you. Last month Dr Wood gently suggested that it might be detrimental to her own physical and mental wellbeing to try again. The walking holiday was intended as a distraction, while we worked out what the rest of our lives might look like. I guess I should be more sensitive.

It is at the garage that we finally see someone. He stands staring at us, a cloth cap pulled down low over his eyes. Straggles of black hair escape over the ridges of his ears. An unkempt moustache where his mouth should be. When we wave he hesitates before lifting his hand, thick fingers clutching a small metal box with wires, and levers, and what appears to be a twisted coat hanger poking out of the top.

'Hello,' I call. 'I wonder if you can help us? We're lost I'm afraid, walking holiday. Is there somewhere we could stay for the night?'

The man scratches at the nape of his neck. Then his moustache twitches.

'I dare say so, aye. We don't get many strangers, but you're welcome. You'll want to talk to P__, he'll set you right. Wait here?'

The coat hanger wags at a wall along the front of the forecourt. As he walks back inside, Debbie and I collapse on to the stonework. I can feel a blister burning under my heel. We lapse into silence.

*

It starts as a purr in the distance, then a grumble, and as the van turns the corner it grows to a throaty roar. When it stops opposite I can see the front bumper, dented and twisted out of alignment, the windscreen crusted with dead insects. One wheel arch is rimmed with a dark red stain, darker than the crimson paintwork.

I almost laugh at the man who steps out. I hear Debbie snort beside me. He's short and stocky, and his nose sticks straight out like the end of a broom handle. His jacket appears to be cut from blue felt, a row of gold-coloured buttons adorning the front, one of them so chipped and faded the plastic shows through. The trousers are of the same material, cut straight without any semblance of fashion or styling. Then there's the hat. It looks like a child's dressing-up outfit, but it's hard to imagine any child wanting to dress as a traffic warden. Sown inexpertly to the front is a Royal Mail badge.

'Well, this is a pleasant surprise,' he says. 'We always welcome new faces around here. T__ tells me you want to stay for the night? How can I help?'

He stands with his back to the van, keeping the road between us. Through the van's window I can see a mangy-looking cat in the front seat, scratching at the upholstery.

'Yes, we're lost I'm afraid. I don't think our map was quite right.' I stand from the wall, hoisting my bag back on to my shoulders. 'But we don't want to put anybody out, we can keep on walking to the next village.'

'No need for that,' he says. 'We're happy to help. That's how we do things around here. There's no hotel as such, but we've a few people away at the moment. My wife has the keys to S__'s old cottage. You'll like it there. How does a hot bath sound? We'll bring you over a lasagne to heat up in the oven.'

Debbie and I share a look. The bath seals it. We hand our bags to the postman and watch him load them into the back of his van.

*

The cottage is simple and rustic, but more than enough for our needs. The ashes in the hearth are laced with a filigree of cobwebs, the bath is furred with a layer of dust, but everything works. On a shelf we find a photo of a middle-aged man, his sideburns growing in two broad stripes down his face, his mouth twisted into something between a smile and a grimace. The picture has been laid flat, face down. There is no other sign of the previous occupant.

As we lie in bed that night, convincing our backs to accept the mattress's lumps and loose springs, Debbie asks me what I make of it all.

'Honestly?' I reply. 'It's a bit weird. But they seem friendly enough, and at least we didn't have to walk another mile today. We'll be gone tomorrow. It'll be a story to tell when we get back home.'

'And the postman?' she asks.

'He's harmless. Small villages are full of eccentrics. I doubt we'll even see him again.'

*

We wake early in the morning, the sun pushing through the thin curtain and flooding the cobwebbed corners of our bedroom. The postman dropped off a selection of miniature boxes of cereal with the previous night's lasagne, all of which are at least two years out of date. Instead we eat oat bars from our walking provisions, assuming that we'll be able to top up with supplies during the day. The instant coffee tastes dusty and weak. Shouldering my bag, I'm already looking forward to a hearty pub lunch on the trail.

When we step outside there is a welcoming committee waiting for us. The moustachioed man from the garage is leaning against a tractor, a stout farmer beside him. He also has a moustache, and I wonder momentarily if they are brothers, or perhaps even lovers. They lift their heads from whatever they've been discussing to stare at us from under their caps.

'P__ has told us to bring you to the village square,' says the taller of the two. 'There's something he wants you to see.'

Debbie tries protesting that we have to hit the road, but the two men are insistent. The tractor starts with a low rumble, like distant thunder. We climb aboard, stowing our packs beneath the seat, and set off through the silent streets.

There are a few others gathered in the square, and as I step down I wonder what they can possibly want. I spot a white ecclesiastical collar on one of the men. That is a comfort, somehow. There is an old lady too, with a shawl wrapped around her shoulders, and four or five unusually quiet children. I see Debbie smile briefly at them. Clearly not a lynch mob to run us out of town, then. They all appear to be waiting for something, their backs against the stone walls of the cottages.

The man from the garage points at a spot on the pavement, and mumbles into his moustache that we are to wait there. It doesn't seem to be something worth making a fuss over, so we do as he says. Perhaps they have arranged a parade in our honour. We wait for several minutes, the vicar nervously checking his watch. It's already past noon. I hope they don't keep us much longer, or the mirage of that pub lunch will disappear.

Then, finally, there is the familiar purr of an engine drawing near. The vicar sighs, and we feel the villagers relax around us. As the postman's van turns the corner they start to cheer. With a crunch of the handbrake he stops in front of us, leaping out of the cab. I'm amused to see that he's still wearing his homemade uniform. It looks so crumpled that I wonder whether he sleeps in it.

'Wait a minute,' he declares with a dramatic sweep of his arm. 'I almost forgot this.'

From the cab he takes a small parcel, wrapped in brown paper and tied up with string. He presents it with a flourish to the vicar. There is no stamp on the front, and where the address should have been there is an illegible scrawl, like a child's approximation of grown-up words.

The vicar smiles. 'Thank you P__, just in time. Well done, I knew we could rely on you. You've saved the day again.'

Debbie looks at me, perplexed, as everyone begins to applaud. The postman capers around in the road, giving everyone a thumbs-up. With a sickening, sinking feeling it occurs to me that this has all been staged for our benefit. The parcel isn't even a real parcel.

I clap when they all turn to stare at us, and do my best to smile. The postman winks. 'Mission accomplished,' he says.

*

The crowd starts to dissipate soon after, and Debbie gives me a look that reflects my own. This is too odd. The sooner we recover our bags, the better. The two moustachioed men have vanished, but we can see the tractor parked at a distance. It is easy enough to swipe our packs, and as we start off along the main road we feel them settle once again on to our backs. I think I see the vicar watching us from the window of one of the cottages, but I may be mistaken. When I look again he is gone.

We try to hurry. My blister has burst overnight and is now an open sore, and my legs are so stiff I can hear one of them creak with every step. But at least we are done with the postman and his strange games. As we limp past the windows of the cottages I try to peer inside. Nobody can be seen in any of them, and most show signs of having lain empty for months, if not years. In one I can make out a photo frame propped up on the mantel, a family of four running hand-in-hand down a golden beach. I'd swear that I've seen it recently in a magazine.

It's only as we near the edge of the village that we notice it. Slight wisps in the air at first, as if there is a fire burning in one of the nearby gardens. Then a distinct haze at the level of the first-floor windows, a soft blanket of gauze laid over the houses. And finally we turn a corner to see a curtain of fog stretched across the road, static and impenetrable, like a wall of sheep's wool.

Debbie looks at me without saying anything. In our condition, in weather like this, there is no way we should be wandering lost in the dales. We managed to get lost even before the fog came in.

Our packs take on an extra weight as we turn and walk back into the village.

*

It's on the third day that someone mentions the bicycle. We've resisted settling into the cottage, but the villagers have made it difficult. They have knocked with homemade meals, hand-baked bread still warm from the oven, fistfuls of wildflowers to cram into dusty vases. They are trying so hard that we can't help wondering about the fog. Neither of us says anything, but the question hangs in the air. The white wall surrounding the village seems thicker with each passing hour.

Debbie is the first to voice our discontent. The postman has gone through his routine again, handing what looks like an empty envelope to the old lady who runs the local shop. Once his cavorting is over, and the crowd is beginning to thin, she speaks to no one in particular.

'I can't believe we're still here,' she says. 'The fog's bad and all that, but am I the only one who finds this ridiculous? Is nobody driving out of town today? We'd be happy to pay someone to borrow their car, if that's what it takes.'

They stare at her as if she's cursed them, or threatened to kill their firstborn while they sleep. There is a leaden stillness to the air that makes it hard to breathe. Then the old lady gathers her shawl about her and speaks.

'There might be a bicycle, I think. Miss H_____ left it behind when she departed. Does anyone know what happened to that?'

The men mutter into their moustaches. The reverend looks at the shiny tips of his shoes.

'We'd be grateful,' I say. 'Really grateful. We're meant to be at work in a couple of days, this was only supposed to be a short ramble. I'd like to get back home.'

The garage mechanic lifts his cap and runs his hand through a thick tangle of hair.

'I'll need to ask P__. Leave it with me, I'll fettle it.'

*

The next morning we wake to a commotion outside. A twitch of the curtains reveals a small crowd. Debbie hurries into the skirt and blouse that one of the women has lent her. I pull on my sweat-stained T-shirt for the fourth day in a row.

When we join them, the reverend grins at us. Several others shoot knowing smiles in our direction. We know better than to ask. Mrs G_____, the old lady from the shop, tugs on Debbie's sleeve.

'Lucky you,' she says. 'It's your turn today. I'm sure you realise how special that is.'

I would laugh, but the time for laughter has passed. Instead I stand and watch the road.

Five minutes later he comes. The scarlet van rounds the corner with a screech, almost tipping over into a bush. When he brakes there is the stink of burnt rubber in the air. As the postman flings open the back doors I am disappointed to see a small brown package sitting on the floor. Not a bike, then. Barely big enough to be a skateboard.

When he reaches us he holds my gaze for a moment longer than normal. I think I see a sneer, although I may have imagined it. As he thrusts the brown paper parcel at me I notice that his hands are unnaturally dry and hard, like untreated wood.

'Looks like I'm just in time,' he says. He looks around at the gathered crowd, pausing for effect. 'Mission accomplished.'

Once the cheers and applause are over and the villagers start to drift away, I am able to sit on the porch step and unwrap the package. It is addressed simply to 'The Strangers'. Instead of a stamp there is a crude drawing of the postman, in profile. I peel back the paper. It takes me a moment to work out what is inside. A rusted bicycle chain, snapped in two places. Several scraps of jerky-like dried meat caught between the links.

There is no note, but the message is clear enough. Once evening falls we pack in earnest.

*

We rise at dawn the next morning, shovelling sticky, stale Frosties into our mouths as we pull on our clothes and shoulder our bags. Although we don't quite understand what is going on, one thing is now clear. We need to be somewhere else.

Debbie has spotted what looks like a train station at one end of the village, and an Indian gentleman who was at the gatherings mentioned a train called the G_____ Rocket. It's a slim hope. The fog still sits around us in dense cotton-wool banks. This village is the entire world.

Creeping through the streets, holding our breath when we can, we almost laugh. As ridiculous as it sounds, part of me expects the post van to come hurtling around the next corner, a magnetic light stuck to its roof, sirens blaring. I had my suspicions on the first day, but now I am sure that the villagers inform Him of our movements. The reverend is certainly in on it, whatever *it* is. And the mechanic. The little old lady from the village shop. Maybe even the kids. What hold He has over them isn't clear, but our parcel hints that it isn't a servitude born of kindness.

When we come to the railway station we find that it is abandoned, of course. Debbie checks the train at the platform while I walk over to the timetable board. It's a meaningless grid of letters and numbers, like a Sudoku puzzle gone horribly wrong. Debbie reports that the train is no better. Simply a hollow shell, empty of anything other than dust and mouse droppings. There is no train, just as there is no mail service. None of it is real.

Holding each other's hand, we clamber clumsily down to the tracks. We can see the exact point where the fog forms at the boundary of the houses. It looks as impenetrable as ever, but at least with the rails beneath our feet we can be certain that we are heading in the right direction. Someone mentioned Pencaster, although any town will do.

When we walk forward into the wall of fog it settles around us, a moist thickness that hugs our bodies and muffles our footsteps. It's like breathing in cotton candy. It's a couple of minutes before we hear the hum in the rails, the faint gleam of a light growing behind us. Then the whistle.

Somewhere in the murk I hear a familiar voice, shouting: 'Special Delivery, on its way.'

Hand in hand, we start to run.

It's true that no man is an island (although some books can be treasure maps), and there are several people without whom this book would never have made it into your hands.

Firstly, and above all else, I have to thank Steve Shaw for taking a punt on a debut collection of decidedly odd stories, and doing so with such generosity and panache. All mistakes in this book are entirely my own – I snuck them in when Steve wasn't looking.

I also have to thank the editors who published some of these stories long before a collection even seemed feasible: Andy Cox, Allen Ashley, Trevor Denyer, C.M. Muller, Robert S. Wilson, John Lavin, Rebecca Parfitt, John Benson, Tim Major, Shona Kinsella, Gary Budden and George Sandison. You're all legends, and your work supporting emerging writers too often goes unnoticed.

Special thanks to Dan Carpenter for agreeing to include our misshapen little collaboration within these pages. And thanks to the Clockhouse Writers and The Talking Cat – without the feedback and advice you offered, several of these stories would have been stillborn.

Finally, thank you to my wife, Hannah, and my sons, Jacob and Ollie. Without them, this book would have been written in half the time. But it wouldn't have been half as good.

Dan Coxon is a Shirley Jackson Award- and British Fantasy Award-nominated editor and author based in London. His stories have previously appeared in *Black Static*, *Nightscript*, *Unsung Stories*, *Not One of Us*, *Unthology* and *The Lonely Crowd*, as well as in the anthologies *Nox Pareidolia*, *Humanagerie* and *Shallow Creek*. His non-fiction has appeared in *The Guardian* and *Salon*. He edited the multi-award-nominated folk-horror anthology *This Dreaming Isle*, as well as the critically acclaimed journal of weird fiction *The Shadow Booth*, and he runs his own proofreading and editing service at momuseditorial.co.uk. A micro-collection of his short fiction, *Green Fingers*, was published by Black Shuck Books in April 2020.

Made in the USA
Las Vegas, NV
10 August 2021

27894183R00106